MAVERICK LAW

They made Thomas Waggoner pick out and saddle his own horse, as the settler still didn't harbor any suspicions that these were anything but bona fide starpackers. DuFran, keeping up the rear, had untied the riata from a saddle thong, and was smiling even as he began fastening a hanging knot.

Elliott took out a pair of handcuffs and said pleasantly to the settler, "Sometimes we've got certain regulations to follow." He made Waggoner rein up, and then Elliott brought the man's arms behind his back to snap on the handcuffs.

To Waggoner's right rode stock detective Fred Coates, who'd kept quiet until now. Clearing his throat, Coates said, "Waggoner, all you are is a mangy horse thief."

"Who are you to pass judgment?" the settler flared back. "You damned lawmen with your tinny little badges are all the same. Say, just where are those badges?"

The answer he received was the rope just cast by Phil DuFran spilling down over his neck.

Coates asked, "Any last words?"

"Just hang the sonofabitch!" chortled DuFran.

BIG HORN HELLRIDERS

ROBERT KAMMEN

ZEBRA BOOKS
KENSINGTON PUBLISHING CORP.

ZEBRA BOOKS

are published by

Kensington Publishing Corp.
475 Park Avenue South
New York, NY 10016

First printing: July, 1991

Printed in the United States of America

One

"Let's hang the sonsofbitches!"

"But one's a woman."

"Along with being a prostitute, Cattle Kate's a receiver of stolen cattle."

"A hanging offense sure enough."

Southerwesterly around the pine-stippled hump of Casper Mountain, and some three miles east of Independence Rock, a man named James Averell ran a road ranch. Averell's place was at the point where the Rawlins-Lander stage line crossed the Oregon trail. He'd hung such titles upon himself as saloonkeeper, postmaster, and justice of the peace. For water there was the Sweetwater River, a stone's throw away from his back porch. Averell's daring to come in here and homestead had made him an enemy of local ranchers.

To set the Carbon County records straight, it was the summer of 1889, with the homestead filed on by Jim Averell in the middle of a huge tract of land claimed by Albert J. Bothwell. Bad blood had sprung up between the rancher and Averell, a former private with the 9th Infantry at Fort McKinney, who upon being discharged in 1881 tried his hand at surveying before turning up in the Sweetwater Valley a scant three years ago.

Just west of Averell's road ranch was a homestead belonging to a woman named Ella Watson. It was said of Ella that she ran a hog ranch, to this end selling her favors to those passing through or local cowhands in exchange for cattle or hard cash. That her neighbor, Averell, had plucked her out of a bawdyhouse in Rawlins. Most of these rumors were being floated about by ranchers in their attempts to drive Ella and her paramour out of the valley. It had even come out in a few newspapers that Ella Watson was a receiver of stolen cattle. Actually the forty head of cattle owned by the woman they now called Cattle Kate were the drags of herds passing through along the Oregon trail, mostly newborn calves which Ella had bought around a dollar a head and was now raising.

More than anything it was Ella Watson's presence over at Averell's saloon that had got people to believing she was a woman of the demimonde. She was a handsome woman, full bosomed and unguarded with her words and smile. That was pretty much all the encouragement a woman-starved cowpoke needed when he rode in for a cold beer. The truth of the matter was James Averell and Ella had been secretly married over at Lander. As to their living on adjoining homesteads, the Homestead Act stated that a married couple could only file on one tract of land. This filing of separate claims had been Averell's idea, and so Ella with his help had put up some buildings on Horse Creek.

As for Jim Averell, not much older than Ella in

his early thirties, he was more educated than most, and had a bantering wit and a growing resentment over the ranchers wanting to increase their grasp on the Sweetwater Valley. More than once he'd had angry words with A. J. Bothwell, as the rancher kept wanting to buy him and Ella out.

"Mostly because we're homesteading along the Sweetwater." From the barroom there came to Averell the murmurings of a few customers. His place was a large log building edging onto the main trail. Through a kitchen window, where he was slicing up a roll of summer sausage, he could see the Crowder boy dropping the potato he'd just pealed into a galvanized tub. A free noon lunch was standard fare at Averell's road ranch, and oftentimes his customers left letters or parcels which were picked up by the stage coach driver on his way to Rawlins.

During the peaceful summer afternoon Averell presided over his barroom, dispensing drinks and keeping up a running conversation with folks he knew. Around four o'clock the shadow of John De Corey fell upon the log plank floor as he came in. He went over to the open end of the bar and said:

"Buchanan showed up." De Corey was a cowboy presently employed by Ella Watson, and he also tended bar, which was the reason he removed his hat and came behind the bar. "You jack up the price on Four Roses?"

"No, John, and there's some sausage and greens out in the kitchen in case you get hungry. I'll be back around ten."

Leaving by the front door, Averell untied the reins of the horse De Corey had ridden over and climbed into the saddle. He was hatless, with the slight breeze tugging at his dark brown hair and ruffling his white shirt. He walked the bronc across the rutted trail and followed a fence line toward the sun-encrusted buildings belonging to Ella Watson. Behind the wire fence some of the mixed assortment of white face and Hereford cattle stirred at his approach, and then Ella's dog, a brindle-haired mix of terrier and some unknown breed, was yapping out at him. Keeping to a walk, he rode up to the small pole corral as cowpuncher Frank Buchanan rose from where he'd been sitting talking to Ella on the front porch. Ambling over, Buchanan, a sandy-haired man with a pleasant smile of greeting for Averell, opened the corral gate as he said, "Couldn't ask for a nicer day."

"Wind's just about right," agreed Jim Averell as he lifted the saddle away and let the bronc trot into the corral. He draped the saddle over a corral pole, stepped with Buchanan toward the house. "Frank, you still thinking of getting into the ranching business?"

"Under this new setup it's too much of a hassle."

Buchanan was all too aware that this new Maverick Law was a ploy of the cattle kings to keep men like him, a cowhand, or even ranch foremen, from starting spreads of their own. He could go out and slap his brand on a maverick, but in so doing would be branded a rustler. All of this was controlled from Cheyenne, where the Wyoming Stock Growers' Association was headquartered. The association, both Buchanan and Jim Averell knew, had range detectives spread throughout the territory. To keep on the lookout for rustlers, which in the parlance of the hard-liners dictating policy for the association meant the small independent rancher or plain cowhand.

Anyone attempting to buck the no-owning rule was blacklisted. Which Frank Buchanan knew would happen to him if he heated up his branding iron.

"Yup, Jim, I guess you and Ella know how it feels to be called rustlers."

For five years running Jim Averell had tried to register his brand over at Rawlins. Blocked at this by a committee lorded over by the cattle kings, this spring he had simply put his brand on the cattle roaming about in Ella Watson's pasture. His reason for doing so was that rancher Albert Bothwell had claimed that these cattle were actually mavericks and legally the property of the stockmen's association. A blatant attempt by Bothwell, Jim Averell knew, to come in and take the cattle. Now he came onto the porch with Buchanan and claimed one of the empty chairs as Ella Watson came to stand in the open front doorway.

"Tough day, Jim?" Ella Watson had on a full calico dress buttoned at her neck and with long sleeves. She'd just combed out her flowing chestnut hair, and stood there while fussing with a bobby pin, and with a smile for both of them. She looked older than twenty-eight, as a few lines had etched themselves around her eyes and mouth. But at the moment there was a deep contentment in her eyes. Ella, like Jim Averell, had heard all the stories bantered about as to their character and had come to accept this, since to reveal that they were married would see her having to give up her homestead. If that happened, without question rancher Bothwell would claim the land back, and maybe Jim's place too. The only true friend they had was Frank Buchanan, and he was also the only person in the Sweetwater Valley who knew they were married. The truth of this was recorded over at Lander. As for Buchanan, they counted themselves so very lucky to have as a friend a person of such impeccable honesty and conviction about his own character. Unlike the harsh stories spread about her, Ella Watson did not allow the drinking of hard liquor at her small log cabin, but would on occasion have something to drink at Jim's place. She knew that her presence over there brought in customers, but this was a hard land of few women, a lonely place where strangers and friends were welcome.

"Supper's on," she announced.

"I appreciate the invite, Ella."

"Back at my pa's farm in Kansas I helped cook for many a threshing crew."

Easing onto a chair in the small kitchen, Frank Buchanan said, "I was never cut out for that farming life."

"Guess I wasn't either," she said with a faraway glimmer in her eyes.

At his place at the table, Jim Averell still had on his mind the news the stage coach driver had told him this afternoon about sighting ranchers R. B. Connor and Albert Bothwell earlier in the day, the ranchers heading off the main trail and taking one that would bring them to the 71 Quarter Circle ranch. This was John Clay's outfit, the ranch headquarters located on the Sweetwater near the historic Three Crossings. If he'd heard right, John Clay was the new president of the stockmen's association, with the ranch being managed by George B. Henderson, and both men avowed enemies of the homesteader and hard-scrabble rancher. As there are few secrets out here, he knew that Henderson was a Pennsylvanian, had been a member of that state's coal and iron police, and once upon a time had been a Pinkerton. With these credentials Jim Averell knew that Henderson was just the kind of man John Clay would hire. The fact the ranchers were getting together brought fresh worries to Jim Averell.

Sipping at the coffee Ella had just poured into his cup, he thought about those ranchers, and that brought to mind a letter of his that had appeared in the *Casper Mail* in early April of this year. A man well versed in prose, Jim had detailed of how the cattle kings out here in the Sweetwater Valley, a mere handful, were just land grabbers camped out as speculators under the Desert Land Act. That none of these men were willing to give up land to settlers or wanted any settlements springing up. It was this letter more than anything, Jim Averell realized, which had set all the ranchers against him. But his fears now, as his eyes lifted to Ella claiming a chair at the table, were for the woman he'd claimed as a wife.

Lately he had come to regret their decision to keep their marriage a secret. Sure, they had this extra land along the creek, but at what price? It had meant Ella's being branded a whore and cattle thief. Though she wasn't one to complain about this setup, he knew it was getting to her, and to him as well. And tonight, as he'd felt for some time, there was this vague sense of unrest. That trouble was coming, and if it came, it would be brought out here to the Sweetwater by Bothwell. Publicly the rancher had stated he meant to drive out both Averell and the whore Cattle Kate. He knew Bothwell to be an arrogant and ruthless man, that the days of idle threats were over.

11

"Remember, Frank, how it was at Christmas . . ."

Puzzled eyes swung to Jim Averell.

"Your saying grace." Averell draped his hand over Ella Watson's.

Bowing his head, Frank Buchanan said, "Reckon I can oblige with a few words of prayer."

Two

The absence of John Clay at his 71 Quarter Circle ranch had given Clay's foreman, a Pennsylvanian named George B. Henderson, an opportunity to speak his mind concerning what was happening along the Sweetwater. Last night Henderson had laid it out plain to Albert J. Bothwell and the other ranchers that the stockmen's association would back up their play.

"We have the newspapers on our side."

"Guess you're right," Albert Bothwell said skeptically, "about keeping John Clay's name out of this. As he does head up the association."

They had just reached Three Crossings, which connected with the stagecoach road, to draw up in a ragged circle, and though all of this had been discussed last night, Tom Sun and a couple of other ranchers were still undecided what to do about Jim Averell. It was Sun wanting to just run Averell out of the Sweetwater Valley, but he or the others hadn't been able to sell this idea to hardheaded Albert Bothwell.

From the seat of his buggy R. B. Conner peered from under bushy brows at the foreman of the 71

Quarter Circle ranch. Seated to Conner's left was rancher Ernest McLain, and now Conner said, "Once this is over, George, we'll telegraph you from Rawlins. And I have to agree with Bothwell that just taking a whip to Jim Averell isn't enough punishment."

"There's the whore, Cattle Kate. Didn't we agree before to hang the pair of them." Albert Bothwell slapped an impatient hand against the neck of his gelding. "You just make sure, Henderson, that you take care of things in Cheyenne. After all, John Clay and a helluva lot of other ranchers are gonna reap the rewards of this. Gents, I suggest we make tracks for Averell's place."

"Now Ella, these Arapaho don't have anything I want."

"How do you know they're Arapaho, John?"

"Don't know what they are," admitted John De Corey as the wagon he was driving bounced over some rough ground angling down toward the river. Behind them about a half-mile they could still make out the Crowder boy in Ella's pasture, making a go at catching one of her ponies.

Coming to the road passing southward toward Independence Rock, Ella Watson touched her hired hand on the arm while gazing uptrail, and she said nervously, "I believe one of them is Albert Bothwell."

"Yup, know the others too," said De Corey as he reined up just short of the main road and held there as the ranchers passed but leaving dark speculating looks for Ella Watson. "Maybe we should head back to your place, Ella? Or maybe

14

head down to Jim's?"

"Bothwell is just an old windbag," she replied. "Come on, John, I've been wanting some Indian beadwork."

De Corey brought the wagon clattering across the road and back onto prairieland and the Indian encampment spread along the Sweetwater. Soon they lost sight of the road and just where those riders had gone, though from the way De Corey drove, Ella Watson knew he was worried, as she was. De Corey stayed in the wagon he'd brought under a shading cottonwood as the woman he worked for got out, with the dogs encircling the wagon being called off by an old Indian buck taking his ease in the shade of a tepee. Usually Ella Watson liked to haggle when buying anything, to take her own sweet time about it, but just seeing Albert Bothwell again, and riding by so brazenly, had brought up her temper. She paid what a squaw was asking for a pair of moccasins, tarried long enough to buy a little beadwork, then she was back in the wagon and urging De Corey to set a faster pace back to her homestead.

"That Bothwell sure gets to you, Ella."

"He's a selfish old man. Wanting everything . . . that me and Jim have worked to get. Dammit, John, all we've got is a few acres while Bothwell's got practically this whole valley."

Once the ranchers had sighted Ella Watson and her hired hand going to the Indian encampment, at Albert Bothwell's orders they had kept to the stagecoach road, and then pulled off as Jim Averell's road ranch lay just over the next elevation of land. Palavering briefly, the ranchers had cut to the west and onto Ella Watson's small tract of homestead. It was John Durbin getting out his riata and using it to pull down the wire fence. Riding on in, he drove the cattle out and hazed them farther to the west before joining up with the other ranchers just closing in on the few buildings belonging to Ella Watson.

"Boy," called out Bothwell to fourteen-year-old Gene Crowder viewing the ranchers from inside the pole corral, "just stay in there and you won't get hurt. Awright, we'll keep out of sight until Ella shows."

The men on horseback and Connor in his buggy found places behind the cabin and the shed, and glancing at Bothwell, John Durbin said:

"Once she notices her cattle have broken out, she might make tracks for Averell's."

"Some of her pasture lays over the hill, so I wouldn't worry about it."

"Been thinking, Albert, what if we just threaten to hang them . . ."

"Reckoned we'd talked ourselves out on that," Bothwell said caustically. "Just driving them off won't keep others from moving in. No, I reckon the die is cast, John, as to what we've got to do."

"They're coming back," Tom Sun announced as he gripped his reins a little shorter. He was more of a rancher than the others, an old-timer out in the Sweetwater Valley, and a man possessed at the moment with hesitations as to why he'd let Bothwell talk him into coming along. Sure, Tom Sun had heard all the stories circulating around about Ella and Jim Averell, knew that a person couldn't separate the straight of it from all the rumors anymore.

They lurked behind the buildings until De

Corey had passed through the last gate, and then with De Corey bringing his wagon and Ella Watson toward her homestead, a word from Bothwell brought them surging out.

The fear of what was happening registered in Ella Watson's voice as she thrust an accusing finger at Albert Bothwell. "How dare you ride in here without an invite!"

"Shut up, you damned hussy," barked Bothwell.

Gathering up her skirts, Ella Watson clambered out of the wagon, only to have Durbin on his bronc and R. B. Conner in his wagon block her progress toward the house, and with Conner telling the woman to get into his wagon.

"I know you, Connor, and I will like hell get into your damned buggy."

"Keep out of this, De Corey," warned Bothwell to the hired hand reaching back for the Winchester. "Just leave that rifle where it is and go into the house. Our quarrel is with Cattle Kate, here." His hard eyes didn't leave De Corey until the man had hurried into the log cabin, then he spurred in close to Ella Watson and lashed the ends of his reins across her face. "You, bitch, get into the buggy."

Ella Watson cried out as she staggered against the buggy wheel, then she asked, "Where are you taking me?"

"To Rawlins," said McLain, who'd gotten out, and now he helped Ella Watson up into the front buggy seat, whereupon McLain climbed into the back seat.

"Can't I at least change clothes?" protested Ella.

"You try making a break for your house and I'll rope and drag you off your place," Bothwell responded. "Now let's get that damned Averell."

John Durbin wheeled his horse around and brought it up to the corral. "Boy, you could get hurt if you decide to get aboard that pony and try warnin' Averell. So just stay put."

Cantering down the clayey lane passing through Ella Watson's homestead, the ranchers swung onto the main road and southward. Some of their uncertainties had gone away now that they'd taken the woman without any trouble, and it seemed as they rode all of them shared Albert Bothwell's contemptuous anger, as the words they bandied about were spoken mostly to bolster the conviction that what they were doing was right and proper, and within the limits of the law.

"What do you know," said Durbin, "here comes Averell in his wagon."

Picking up the pace of their horses, the ranchers closed in on Jim Averell just passing through the second gate on his property. Bothwell, after unlimbering his six-gun, said brusquely, "Elevate your hands, Averell. We have a warrant for your arrest."

"A warrant? Then produce such a document."

"Damn you, nestor, our guns are warrant enough." Rancher Bothwell motioned for Averell to get into the buggy, and with a damning resentment coloring his face, Jim Averell left his wagon there and got into the buggy. To have the ranchers set out immediately in the direction of Independence Rock.

"John," yelled young Gene Crowder, "they're gone!" He swung the corral gate open as De Corey hurried out of the log cabin.

18

"I tell you," said the cowhand, "that Bothwell means to do harm to Ella. All we can do is warn Jim about this." He swung up behind the boy seated aboard the pony, and taking the reins where he occupied the back of the saddle, spurred up the lane.

It was after two o'clock now on this sultry Saturday afternoon of a July 20th, and it took De Corey nearly a half-hour to reach Jim Averell's road ranch, out in front of which a few horses were idling. He leaped down and let Crowder tend to the pony, to shoulder through the partly opened door and into the barroom, and with the cowhand's voice breaking as he said loudly:

"They took Jim and Ella . . . Bothwell and some other ranchers got them. Bothwell's heading for the Rock."

"Jim just left here," said Frank Buchanan. "Well, come on. We just can't let Bothwell have his way with them."

Frank Buchanan broke for the front door before it came to him that everyone was just standing there, and he swung back to face men he knew.

"Look, Frank, they probably won't harm Jim and Ella . . ."

"Yeah, just want to throw a scare into them."

The probing eyes of Frank Buchanan took it all in, their fear of the ranchers, and that by bucking Albert Bothwell, any one of them could receive like treatment. But there wasn't time at the moment to build up any resentment toward these men, nor did they seem aware of the situation as he saw it. This time the ranchers were playing for keeps, which to him could only mean a rope for Jim Averell and Ella being hustled out of the valley. He spun away through sawdust and found the front door and his horse tethered outside, and with not even a glance for ashen-faced Gene Crowder still sitting his pony.

At a gallop he brought his bronc straight toward the low hump of Independence Rock. The sun was out and blinding to the eye. And it wasn't until Frank Buchanan brought his horse around a jumbled pile of rocks and spotted the ranchers making for the west end of Independence Rock that it suddenly occurred to him all he had for a weapon was his Colt .45. That in all likelihood the ranchers would be packing Winchesters.

"Can't worry about that now," he muttered. "As I've got real bad feelings about this all because of Albert Bothwell."

The ranchers brought their horses into the shallow waters of the ford and went splashing up the bed of the Sweetwater. The buggy driven by R. B. Connor had a harder time of it, and he was forced to slow his horses down, but two of the ranchers hung in behind the buggy just in case their prisoners tried to get away.

About two miles downriver Albert Bothwell, riding next to John Durbin out in front of the buggy, decided to stop and parley, and he drew up and pulled around so suddenly that his horse shouldering into Durbin's almost dislodged Durbin from his saddle. Bothwell made no excuses about this as he said:

"Think we're being followed?"

"Chances are we're not," said R. M. Galbraith. "That Crowder kid and Ella's hired hand are still shaking in their boots."

Jim Averell, until now nursing his resentful

silence, said, "Generally anyone serving a warrant takes his prisoners to a jail. What's your game, Bothwell?"

"You damned fool," swore the rancher, "this is no game. You damned nestors come in here and hog all my water . . . just steal land belongin' to me . . . and you call it a game."

"We filed legal-like on that land," cried out Ella Watson.

"You . . . slut." Bothwell raised his arm as if to strike the woman, only to have Tom Sun crowd in and have his horse edge Bothwell's away from the buggy.

"Hitting a woman, no matter who it is, goes against the grain, Bothwell."

"What about it, Ella, you either leave the country or this water's deep enough to drown in."

"Leave her be," said Jim Averell as he stared at the woman he'd married gazing back at him. The truth had to come out about them, he realized. For he saw in the eyes of these men that they were set upon a hanging. He scarcely believed even now that any harm would come to Ella.

"Yeah, Cattle Kate, we just made you an offer—"

"Listen up," interrupted Averell. "Because what they say about Ella isn't true. Ella and I—"

"No, Jim, don't tell them anything!" she yelled.

"Enough of this," cut in Albert Bothwell. "No more damned sass from the two of you. Truth you said, Averell. The truth is you're a whoremaster an' rustler besides. We've got a job to do, so let's head out."

The lynch mob of six ranchers brought their horses into motion, with John Durbin pointing ahead to the hidden recesses of Spring Creek canyon. "Plenty of trees in there."

"It'll do," came Bothwell's grim response.

Sometime later they broke into the canyon, which lay about five miles above Averell's road ranch. Now they halted to give their horses a breather and to bind the arms of their captives. In the canyon they found rocks and sagebrush and scrub timber, and with the screening walls to either side, they felt more certain of what they were about to do. Heading out again, it was Durbin riding point by his lonesome as Albert Bothwell held up to ride alongside the buggy.

"Averell, that was damned stupid of you not selling out when given the chance."

"You know, Bothwell, you're a pig . . . just rooting around in the dirt in hopes of finding another acorn . . . but all the time all you come up with is more cow shit."

Blinded by Averell's damning words and his own anger, the rancher clawed out his handgun. He brought the barrel raking across Jim Averell's face to slice his left cheek open and draw blood. "Get those ropes on these damned thieves!"

A couple of the other ranchers grabbed Averell's arms and pulled him off the buggy seat as Galbraith coming in from behind managed to drop his looped rope over their victim's head and snug the noose tight around Averell's neck. They brought Averell up to a ledge and a pine growing there, and it was here that Galbraith tossed the other end of the rope up over a low branch.

Down at the buggy, McLain was having some difficulty trying to put his rope around Ella Watson's neck as she kept dodging her head and screaming. "Damn it, give me a hand with her." Then with the help of John Durbin, they pulled

Ella out of the buggy and brought her still struggling and crying out up the slope.

"Come on," Bothwell said tauntingly to Jim Averell, "be a gamer and jump off."

Averell kicked out at his tormentor and shouted, "I'm not going to die that easy, you murderin' pig!"

"Jim!" Ella screamed. "Help me!"

Both of them kept struggling against the efforts of the ranchers to end their lives up here on this summit of a cliff fronting the Sweetwater River. Then to the surprise of the ranchers, someone opened up with a six-gun, and in the confusion they scattered down to their horses and their sheathed Winchesters as more leaden slugs scoured the rocks around them.

"Back there!"

"Can you make out who it is?"

"Nope," said Durbin as he pivoted sideways from where he crouched behind a few scrub trees and took in Albert Bothwell watching over their prisoners. He swung back and glanced at Ernest McLain. "But I figure whoever it is isn't packing a rifle. Let's work in closer."

Farther back in the canyon Frank Buchanan reloaded his Colt as the return fire coming from the ranchers seemed to be getting closer. His eyes still held the shock of what he'd seen, Jim and Ella up on that ledge with ropes around their necks.

"There's Bothwell up there. But the others, Durbin, Sun, Connor, just aren't the kind to do something like this." Desperately he emptied his Colt again, not scoring any hits, and knowing that he had no chance against those Winchesters. Only when Frank Buchanan had used up all the bullets in his gunbelt did he break back to his horse.

When John Durbin heard the thud of hoofbeats retreating down the canyon, with McLain at his side he went back to their horses, as did the others. Upon focusing their attention on the ledge, they discovered that Albert Bothwell had shoved both of their victims over the ledge, but that Jim Averell and Ella Watson were still moving.

"That's only about a two-foot drop," Durbin said disgustedly.

"Meaning instead of hanging them we're strangling them to death."

"One way or other the job is done."

Hearing a horse whicker, some of them swung around to see Tom Sun riding away, and it was McLain who said wonderingly, "Tom never did help with the ropes . . . or use his rifle for that matter."

"Don't worry, you can count on Sun to still be siding with us. Well, it's over for the whore Cattle Kate and her paramour. Let's go."

"What about Bothwell?"

"Knowing him, he'll stay up there to make sure of things."

And the ranchers left, all but Albert J. Bothwell, up on that ledge and still throwing curses at those he hated.

The sight of Frank Buchanan coming in at a gallop brought everyone out of Jim Averell's road ranch. The words came out hard from Buchanan. "They hung both Ella and Jim."

There seemed to be no response from the customers of Jim Averell, as there was no offer of any of them to make that long ride into Casper with Frank Buchanan to get the sheriff. Wasting no more time or words, Frank Buchanan simply reined his horse away from the tie rail and headed it northerly.

During the night of his long ride, Buchanan got lost riding through Albert Bothwell's big pasture, and hours later he managed to find the trail again. It was around three o'clock that he swung off his exhausted horse at Tex Healy's homestead shack, which was about twenty-five miles from the Sweetwater and a like distance to Casper. A light showed first, then Healy came out to be told of the tragedy back along the Sweetwater.

"I knew there'd be trouble, Frank. But to hang a woman . . ."

"I figure, Tex, this is just the start of it. The ranchers are out for blood . . . and the good Lord have mercy on anyone standing in their way."

Three

Although Tex Healy brought news of the hanging into Casper just before noon on Sunday, it wasn't until Monday that a posse headed for the Sweetwater Valley. They found the victims of the ranchers still hanging from the limb of a stunted pine, their arms touching, their faces swollen almost beyond recognition.

At the same time, George Henderson was holding court on the front porch of the Cheyenne Club. In Henderson's words, he had just happened to be in the capital when news of the hanging had been telegraphed to him from Rawlins. Peering through the curtained windows at the reporters eagerly hanging on every word uttered by the foreman of the 71 Quarter Circle ranch were some ranchers. Another interested spectator was idling across the street, Major Frank Wolcott, a charter member of the stockmen's association.

George Henderson was a big man, and for this occasion had donned a suit and fancy vest. He had a habit of flicking his right hand around when talking. He'd shed his gunbelt, and his coat was open, showing a roll of fat bulging out over his belt.

"By reputation Averell was a murderous coward," expounded Henderson. "The woman was no better . . . an' could sit a horse better'n some I know."

"Wasn't she known as Cattle Kate?"

"Hard to believe she rustled cattle."

"Damn right she did," spoke up another of these news toadies clustered around George Henderson.

"Gents, it's hot . . . and I'm about talked out."

"Just who did hang Averell and the woman?"

"This telegram doesn't give any names. My guess is it was some honest folks taking the law into their hands. You can bet the Sweetwater will be a better place after this." With a placating smile for the reporters, Henderson found the nearest door and went into the Cheyenne Club.

He left behind the reporters scattering away and Major Frank Wolcott crossing toward the club, while still lingering on the steps was James Haskins, who'd been sent out here by the *Chicago Gazette* about three weeks ago to check out these stories about rustling. The ranchers had been more than willing to be interviewed by Haskins, youngish and with a crooked grin belying pondering brown eyes. To a man, the cattle kings had pointed accusing fingers at those just getting into the cattle business, even some who worked for them, and the small rancher. The other faction called these cattle kings the feudal lords of Wyoming, and a lot more names that Haskins had been unable to use in his stories. But one of the pieces of information he did come across was of a recent bad winter killing off a lot of cattle left to drift for themselves until spring. Before this, investors from back East and Europe had been more than willing to invest in or buy a ranch of their own. Sometimes an eager buyer succumbed to a book rather than a head tally, and forked out ready cash for five thousand head of cattle whereas all he'd purchased was half that number. Padded accounts were kept by many a ranch manager, an accepted practice. To justify the loss of cattle during that bad winter, and his crooked bookkeeping, many a cattleman cried out . . . rustler! And, James Haskins had also discovered, since these cattle kings controlled most of the newspapers in Wyoming, the cry of rustler was picked up again and again.

Now, he mused, the sordid story of Cattle Kate and the killer Jim Averell would make front-page news in Denver, Omaha, and St. Louis. Was it a coincidence that George Henderson just happened to be here to pick up that telegram? And just who had sent it? This all seemed so contrived, Haskins thought as he strolled downstreet toward the privacy of a saloon, there to soak up some cold beer and ponder over just what kind of story he would send to his newspaper.

"Henderson, I suspect, was playing a pat hand. For I also suspect someone involved in the hanging sent that telegram. As for the Cheyenne Club, Henderson is in there now being congratulated by those really behind this whole thing. He's just one of the court jesters. The real power men are Major Wolcott, Guernsey, and of course, John Clay."

His mind still sorting out what had just taken place, James Haskins entered the Golden Saloon, there to jot down the bare bones of his editorial before he caught the morning stage for Casper. Here in Cheyenne anything of importance that happened was whitewashed by the stockmen's association and the cattle kings. In Casper, Doyle was hoping, he would find out if what happened to Cattle Kate was justifiable homicide or cold-blooded murder.

"The position of the association, George, is that we cannot make a visible show of support for Albert Bothwell and the other ranchers."

"It was Bothwell more than the others wanting to get rid of Averell and that woman," said George Henderson.

Major Frank Wolcott cupped a hand around his glass and said, "I assume John Clay explained our position."

"My boss did exactly that. Which was the chief reason, Major Wolcott, I didn't go with them to Averell's place."

"There'll be witnesses to what happened, I expect. So when you get back, please tell Mr. Bothwell and our other good friends that we have people who can handle the situation."

"Major, it's been a pleasure," said George Henderson as he flashed a smile that took in the others occupying the table, and rising, he left the room.

Occupying a chair at the head of the table was Major Frank Wolcott, by description somewhat chunky and not all that tall. He had the sour mash drawl of a Kentuckian, though Wolcott had served on the Union side during the Civil War. His eyes matched the cynical smile below the brown mustache, and he had a strong jaw that closed with a snap after every sentence he uttered. It was Sheriff Malcolm Campbell of nearby Converse County who'd spoken of the major as being a cocky bantam rooster, a man known to cheat his hired hands out of their wages and someone detested by most of his neighbors. Despite all this, he was a polished gentleman, which was probably the reason the cattle kings accepted the major as an equal.

To Wolcott's right sat the garrulous H. B. Ijams, the new secretary of the Wyoming Stock Growers' Association. It was through Ijams's office that stories which had been rubberstamped by association president John Clay were released to the newspapers. Boldly he let it be known in this manner as to who was being blackballed for defying the infamous Maverick Law. And with vengeance of purpose had Ijams sent out association detectives to spy out the activities of small ranchers, or anyone else trying to get into the business of raising cattle. In his possession at all times was a small leather valise containing paperwork that required his immediate attention. One of the laws which had been passed on to H. B. Ijams was one forbidding any rancher to employ any man owning a brand or cattle, and as secretary he would often cite the gist of this law at association meetings.

The others were ranchers, plain and simple, some just in visiting, but many had taken to living in Cheyenne, by putting up sumptuous houses so they could enjoy the good life offered by the Cheyenne Club and to rub elbows with their own kind. Conspicuously absent was John Clay, away in Denver, as explained by Major Frank Wolcott.

One of the ranchers passed gas.

Guffaws registered around the table, with one rancher ordering a round of drinks, this barked to a mulatto servant.

"Gentlemen," Major Frank Wolcott said after the laughter had subsided, "it seems we have a moment of crisis."

"Crisis hell, Wolcott, some rustlers were hung is all."

"I'll drink to that."

"Yup, here's to Bothwell and McLain and those others . . ."

Prominent among the ranchers gathered around the table was Charles A. Guernsey, a stockman and longtime member of the Cheyenne Club. Guernsey had just sent a story to *Wyoming Cowboy Days* stating that he approved of the lynching. Directly across the table sat Teschemacher, the owner of a large ranching operation at Bridger's Ferry on the North Platte. Teschemacher exercised considerable influence as a member of the association's executive committee. Jug-eared and stony-faced, Hubert Teschemacher had yet to comment about the recent hangings; his presence at this table was at the insistence of Major Wolcott. A Harvard graduate, he was wealthy and widely traveled. Now Teschemacher drummed impatient fingers on the oaken table as those ranchers not on the committee began rising to take their departure.

Remaining in the room were Secretary Ijams, and along with Guernsey and Teschemacher one William C. Irvine, on the committee and owner of the Converse Cattle Company which lay east of Powder River in that Antelope Creek and Cheyenne River country. At Irvine's elbow reposed a snifter of brandy while cigar smoke curled up past the mustachioed, sunburnt face and over the thatch of thinning black hair. He supported without question the actions of the secretary and Major Wolcott, and realized as did Teschemacher that something other than news of the recent hanging had brought about this meeting. He coughed, then twisted in his high-backed chair and hacked phlegm into a gleaming brass cuspidor.

"So it seems it has begun," Major Frank Wolcott announced. He met approving eyes around the table.

This was a man, this arrogant Frank Wolcott, who had been enticed out to Territorial Wyoming by then President Ulysses S. Grant to take over as Receiver of Public Monies, U.S. Land Office. Later on he served as a U.S. marshal and also warden of the federal prison at Laramie City. Throughout his blustery and oftentimes underhanded activities as a federal official, he had seen the livestock industry grow from small herds of Texas Longhorns to enormous herds grazing across Wyoming's seemingly endless free government grass. After Wolcott's dismissal from federal service, he cannily established a ranch on Deer Creek about four miles from its mouth on the Platte, which placed it in the heart of the Fort Fetterman Hay Reservation. From the front porch of the spacious ranch house he put up, Major Wolcott could take in Deer Creek Valley and the cloud-enshrouded Laramie Mountain Range. Then came the winter of death and Wolcott and most of the ranchers in Wyoming lost most of their cattle. This brought Frank Wolcott to the wall, and heavily in debt, he lost his Deer Creek ranch. Wolcott didn't give up but filed to receive a homestead patent for a parcel of land near Glenrock. It was from here that the major, desperate now and in a vengeful frame of mind, managed to convince some of the larger ranchers to join him in a plot to get rid of the rustlers infesting their territory.

"What have you come up with, Frank?"

"A list of names, Mr. Irvine," said Wolcott, and Secretary Ijams reached into his valise and brought out a large yellow sheet of paper, which Ijams placed on the table for all to see.

In a bland tone of voice, Teschemacher said, "Call it what it really is, Major Wolcott—a death list."

William Irvine leaned forward to see better and ran his eyes down the list of names. "Most of them seem to reside in Johnson County."

"A county overrun with rustlers, I can assure you."

"Consider this, gentlemen," said Guernsey. "I'm absolutely certain warrants will be issued for the arrest of those who hung this woman, Cattle Kate, and Averell. We're all in agreement that they were rustlers. So here's the rub. Our friends over at Sweetwater are big ranchers. And once a jury is impounded, which I'm sure will be made up of the working class, there could be a guilty verdict."

"I have to agree," said Wolcott. "But, Mr. Guernsey, we have the means to handle this."

"Yes, I suppose we do," interrupted Teschemacher. "Do we really want to get the association involved in this? If found out, well, we have our enemies."

To which Secretary Ijams said, "I suggested to George Henderson that ours will merely be an advisory role. Henderson said there were witnesses to the hanging."

"Whatever," said Teschemacher. "Getting back to your list, Wolcott. The name of the Johnson County sheriff is here, and other officials up there at Buffalo."

"Sir, all of these men are arrayed against us. They resist our trying to enforce the Maverick Law . . . shelter, I might add, known rustlers. As the Romans once did, we must wipe out these men when we invade Johnson County."

"If we invade Johnson County," cut in Guernsey. He was sometimes appalled by Major Wolcott's complete absence of tact, had even spoken to some of the association members in regard to having Wolcott removed from his job as assistant to John Clay, the association president. Only to be outvoted, for most of the cattle kings enjoyed having Wolcott speak out for them.

"That is still open to debate."

Guernsey speared Secretary Ijams with an impatient glance, and he said, "Yes, we have a lot of influence in the governor's office, and even have a clear line of communication right up to the White House. However, before we do anything about Wolcott's death list, I suggest we wait and see just what happens to our friends up in the Sweetwater. It just might be that public opinion throughout Wyoming sides with Albert Bothwell and the others. If this proves out, then we act accordingly."

Teschemacher rising from his chair was a signal that the meeting was over, even though Major Frank Wolcott thought otherwise. Wolcott left the Cheyenne Club in the company of H. B. Ijams to return to the association offices in downtown Cheyenne. Plying a deck of cards in a game of solitaire was association detective Ben Morrison, his wide, low-crowned hat perched on a chair, and he had a drooping handlebar mustache, careful eyes that judged Wolcott to be in one of his foul moods. He laid the cards down as Ijams and Wolcott heaved onto chairs at the table. As was

Morrison's habit, he would let the others open the conversation, which Ijams promptly did in a caustic way.

"About all we established over there was that two people were hanged. Can't our people understand just how urgent the situation is."

"Most of them," said Wolcott, "are old horse traders. Probably the reason they are wealthy. But"—he picked up a card, the ace of spades— "there are ways to circumvent association bylaws."

"The reason I'm here?"

"Yes, Ben. I want you to head up to Casper. Find out what actions the sheriff up there has taken. Then go over to the Sweetwater and get together with Bothwell . . . and it wouldn't hurt to talk to George Henderson."

"As you mentioned earlier, major, there were witnesses to what happened. I'm figuring even if these ranchers are charged with murder, well, you know what I mean."

"We certainly do," said Ijams. "I don't believe we can be a party to what you seem to be suggesting."

"What we can suggest," said Wolcott, "and what I want you to tell those ranchers, Ben, is that we are in the right. Witnesses can be bribed, if that becomes necessary, or—"

Ben Morrison interjected, "Or they can disappear. Knowing the sheriff up there, he'll bring those ranchers in to stand trial."

"They'll be released on bond," said Major Wolcott. "Now to this Johnson County thing. More and more our members have come to agree with me that we must take action against this rustling. I've discussed with some of them the need to bring in hired guns."

H. B. Ijams said, "But not until we find out which way the wind blows up at Casper. A jury could come up with a guilty verdict. The law—"

"We are the law!" Major Wolcott's jaw snapped shut, to snap open again. "We have the money and the power and the courts behind us. Gentlemen, we are going to invade Johnson County. But as you say, Ijams, we can't do so without the tacit approval of the executive committee."

"Joe Elliott had an idea." Elliott was an association detective and stock inspector working in northeastern Wyoming. Ben Morrison stroked his mustache as he added, "Supposin' we were to serve a warrant on someone on that list of yours, Major Wolcott. Doesn't mean, as Elliott told me, this rustler would ever see the inside of a jail. Just arrest him . . . and leave him dangling from some tree."

"Vultures picking away at a man hanging from a tree is a powerful message that we mean business. We'll keep it under discussion, Ben. Meanwhile, take care of this Casper business."

"Yup, I'll mosey up there." Languidly he reached for his hat and rose to leave the room, at which time Ijams said, "What do you think of Elliott's idea?"

Major Frank Wolcott replied, "I like it. It should serve notice to the rustlers as to our intentions. But our real enemies are up in Johnson County. Frank Canton's up there. Summon Canton and some of our other men here to Cheyenne. I believe it's time they saw the names on our death list. Yes, I believe the time of the rustler is about over in Wyoming."

Four

A couple of days ago a man would have given his best horse and a night on the town just for a dipperful of rainwater. What anyone hadn't expected was this cloudburst, gully washing upon the cowtown of Buffalo. The swollen waters of Clear Creek were threatening to wash out the Main Street bridge and the Occidental Hotel just to the north. A drunk reeling out of Zindel's choked off a frightened cry for help upon realizing it was a goat being tumbled and churned downstream and not a naked woman. The drunk promptly fell into the eely mud of the street.

The cloudburst served to bring a lot of people into the cafés and saloons, where under discussion was the tragedy down along the Sweetwater. News of the hanging dislodged from the front page of the *Buffalo Bulletin* stories about another company of soldiers being pulled out of Fort Mckinney. It was the fort, constructed some twelve years ago, which had seen Buffalo change from a waystation to its present size. Later it was the cattlemen making Buffalo their choice of places to buy supplies or to socialize. Then came the winter of '87, one so terrible with its unrelenting storms that many a rancher went under.

Then in midsummer the Cheyenne Leader came out with editorials accusing Johnson County of harboring organized gangs of rustlers. This was followed up by the stockmen's association black-balling nearly every rancher in the county and a bunch of free-lancing cowboys. The thoughts of Joe DeBarthe were centered on this from where he sat at his desk working on an article for his newspaper, the *Bulletin*.

The rain had slackened up but rainwater still trickled through a crack in the tarred roof and spattered into a pail he'd set on the floor. He looked up from his words scrawled on a yellowed sheet of paper and glanced out a window. He liked being here in this town of Buffalo hugging the eastern slopes of the Big Horns. Mostly he liked rubbing elbows with cowboys and cavalrymen and the few outlaws bold enough to try the many saloons of this cow town.

"Maybe?" deliberated Joe DeBarthe. "Maybe I ought to place on paper what's really going on around here?" What he had it in mind to do was to bring to light the feud between former Johnson County sheriff Frank Canton and John A. Tisdale, a rancher. Or the bad blood Fred Hesse had for Jack Flagg. Likewise Frank Canton was having words with Flagg and with Sheriff Red Angus, who'd beaten him in the last county election. He'd have to include ranch foreman Mike Shonsey holding a grudge against both Flagg and Nate Champion. Finally there were Champion and Flagg, the owner of the Hat outfit, defying the big outfits, whose plans to get even with these men were an ill-kept secret.

Gulping down coffee that had cooled to a bitter tang, the editor of the *Bulletin* knew all of this was wishful thinking. He'd more or less be signing his death warrant if something of this nature ever got into his newspaper. But this was something that De Barthe and everyone else around here had to live with. To someone coming in on the stagecoach Buffalo seemed peaceable enough, greened into summer, an ordinance in force but ignored that no one pack a gun within the city limits.

By early afternoon the clouds were scattering out enough to give anyone poking his head out of a door a glimpse of the mountain shouldering over Buffalo. The air felt crisper, cleaner, but Nate Champion had other things on his mind. Once in a while he would glance over at Jack Flagg standing by a window, Flagg holding there in the hopes he'd spot Frank Canton again.

"Breaking up," said Jack Flagg. "You sure it was Joe Elliott with Canton?"

"It was Elliott," Champion affirmed softly. Sometimes Nate Champion had to be prodded into speaking, and he was stocky and had steely gray eyes. He had earned the respect of most everyone around Buffalo and its neighboring ranches, though there were a few cattlemen he'd rankled because Champion wouldn't back down to anybody. The six-gun thonged down at his right hip was more'n an ornament, as many considered him to be about the fastest gun in Johnson County.

As for the presence of Jack Flagg in Buffalo, the rancher had come in to see one of the bankers, and later he'd stopped off and paid for some more advertisements to be run in the *Buffalo Bulletin*. He owned the notorious Hat ranch in partnership with four other men. The stockmen's association and its aligned cattle kings called these men nothing more than rustlers. Flagg's Hat brand had been registered with the county. And the ads he liked to run in the *Bulletin* showed the likeness of an enormous cowboy hat etched across the ribs of a woodcut steer, these advertisements flaunted insolently alongside those of the respectable outfits.

Unlike the reputation earned by Nate Champion as a fast man with a gun, the weapon used frequently by Jack Flagg was the ability to express himself, having been a schoolteacher at one time. He always wore a black hat, and he was tall and somewhat handsome. Flagg had a passion for fine liquor and gambling. He was outspoken, and possessed a quarrelsome nature.

Jack Flagg's partners in the Hat outfit came from Texas, as did Nate Champion. And all were sworn enemies of the big outfits, though last year Billy Hill had sold out his share of the ranch and struck out for Canada. This was after indictments were brought against the owners of the Hat outfit by the court of the Second Judicial District. All because the partners had defied the boycott placed against them by the stockmen's association. The boycott simply meant that the Hat outfit couldn't eat at the larger outfits' wagons nor expect any help in gathering its cattle during the spring roundup. This failed to deter Jack Flagg, as he and his partners each owned a string of horses and had a team and wagon, and after hiring a cook, they headed out.

A couple of days into the roundup found the Hat outfit working to the south along the South Fork of Powder River, a long finger reaching into the central Wyoming plateau. The other branches of Powder River were to the north, all of them bringing clear mountain waters out of the Big Horns. As expected, the weather was still somewhat chilly, warming into the upper fifties at times, with a wind always coming around mid-morning to stir up dust.

The herd gathered by the owners of the Hat outfit and the few hired hands numbered around a hundred head of cattle and some bulls and steers, but troubling Jack Flagg was that the brands on some of the calves had been blotched.

"They didn't do a good job of it either," groused Tom Gardner, one of those holding a calf down to better read the fresh brand burned into its flank.

"Yup, you can damnsure make out our Hat marking under that damned CY brand." Jack Flagg, anger tightening up his face, realized this was a deliberate act on the part of the CY, which headquartered farther south along the North Platte River. He straightened in the saddle and set his eyes southward on a pallor of dust showing above an elevation. "Shonsey's still foreman?"

"Yeah, Jack, last I heard." Tom Gardner let the calf go bawling away and swung into the saddle. "You got it in mind to pay Shonsey a visit?"

"First they call us rustlers; now the bastards do this. Just you and me and Lou Webb will go."

"The CY won't be expecting us."

"The CY and that maverick-stealing stockmen's association," exploded Flagg, "didn't figure on us bucking their crooked laws."

It took the three cattlemen the rest of the morning to come upon the outer fringes of the large herd being gathered by the CY outfit. Distantly they could see that two branding fires were going, and Jack Flagg brought his horse

43

through bunches of grazing cattle and over prairie churned by the hooves of both cattle and horses. The wind threw dust in their eyes and the stench of fresh cow manure into their nostrils. They had little difficulty spotting foreman Mike Shonsey presiding over one of the branding fires, and now the smile froze on Shonsey's face when he realized it was Jack Flagg.

Though just a foreman, Mike Shonsey had always been an avowed enemy of smaller ranchers such as Jack Flagg and those he called partners. Shonsey was raw-boned, bigger than Flagg just swinging down from his bronc, and quite adept at fisticuffs. He said disdainfully, "You're trespassing on CY land."

"You brand-blottin' sonofabitch!"

The foreman of the CY reeled back under the impact of Jack Flagg's fists slamming into his stomach and cutting along a cheekbone. He was knocked down and just managed to roll away from branding irons flames licking at his shirt. Quickly regaining his feet, Shonsey launched an uppercut that struck Flagg high in the shoulder. Jack fell backward under the sheer viciousness of his assailant's fist, taking a blow to the bridge of his nose that broke it and sent blood spraying over his face as he went down again, barely aware of where he was, but shimmering with hatred.

Before reclaiming his horse, Jack Flagg proclaimed his intentions to Shonsey and the other CY hands clustered around that he would be back to cull out any Hat outfit cattle stolen by the CY ranch.

Out of this encounter with Mike Shonsey and the CY had come the indictments for the owners of the Hat outfit. Only to have them dismissed by the prosecuting attorney for Johnson County. This led to wild charges as to the breakdown of law in the northern reaches of Wyoming by the ranchers and stockmen's association. And at the moment, as Jack Flagg kept an eye out for Frank Canton, he knew that what had just happened along the Sweetwater could take place up here.

He stepped over to share the table with Nate Champion and said, "This is about all the rain we've had for some time. Won't help much as the ground is so dry the rain sinks right in; be bone dry in a couple of days."

"What you're saying, Jack, is that things are coming to a head."

"What I'm mostly saying is that the cattle kings are trying to stop the encroachments of civilization. They seem to liken themselves to feudal lords of old. Where knights and kings as they claim to be ruled without due regard to law or the needs of the peasant, or poor landed gentry such as ourselves. This Cattle Kate thing . . . I'm afraid, Nate, it's just the beginning."

"You said Al rode in?" Nate Champion was inquiring as to the whereabouts of another Hat outfit partner, Texas Al Allison, whose real name was Tisdale.

"His brother's due in from the Dakotas."

"So you told me before."

"Name's John Tisdale—plans to homestead north of me on Red Fork."

The Big Horns had been drawing John Tisdale toward them ever since he pulled out of Belle Fourche a few days back. Up until a month ago he'd managed the Northern Pacific stockyards at

Mandan, in the Dakotas. He was forty and had left a family behind, with the intention of bringing them out here when he got settled onto a homestead. And here for Tisdale was Buffalo, which was revealing itself to be a sizable cow town when he cantered over a rise in the stagecoach road.

Tisdale was a cattleman, pure and simple, and had bossed three herds up from Texas. For a time he'd worked out at Teddy Roosevelt's Maltese Cross ranch in the badlands. Ever since leaving Texas he'd kept in touch with a brother, had in fact advanced money for his brother's entry into the Hat outfit partnership. So to John Tisdale, he was more or less coming to a place where he wouldn't be all that much of a stranger.

As he came in from the east, it was the lush grassland and various creeks and rivers that told John Tisdale this would be a good place to start up a ranch. In the letters Tisdale had received from his brother, and of course the accounts in the newspapers, he knew about the rustling problem out here. That his brother, Al Allison, had made vague mention of the Hat outfit being accused of throwing its brand on mavericks.

"Seems to me," murmured John Tisdale as he came onto Main Street and drew up to rest his horse under some shading trees, "those newspaper stories I've been readin' accuse most everyone in these parts of being rustlers. This place has got a sheriff, county commissioners, and that court-house yonder. Something just don't smell right."

He drew rein in front of the Occidental Hotel, which to John Tisdale was a lot more hotel than he expected for any struggling cow town. His view of the long facade and the orderly lay to Main

Street served to chase away some lingering doubts as to his coming out here to start a new life. The creek gushing by under the bridge brought a thirsty whicker from one of the horses. But Tisdale's first order of business was finding a bank to deposit the money he'd been packing along, and tying up, he nodded civilly to some passing soldiers before entering the lobby of the Occidental Hotel.

He inquired about a room, told the clerk he would register later, and was told about the town having two banks, with the clerk going on to enlighten the newcomer to Buffalo about this ordinance concerning the holstered sidearm of Tisdale's. "But sir," the clerk related further, "a lot of folks hereabouts just keep on packing their sidearms."

Ambling outside, the former Texan kept to shadows fringing along the hotel as he took a closer look at the town. Main Street dipped southward toward the creek, and beyond the bridge the narrow street crept upward. Like the Occidental Hotel, there were a few brick-fronted buildings, among them the saloon directly across the way, the bank owned by Stebbins & Conrad, and the Q.T. Bowling Alley. Among other items related to him by the desk clerk was of the livery stable connected to the hotel, and now John Tisdale brought his horses around to the back to leave them in care of a hostler.

Tisdale had just rambled back to Main Street with the idea of opening a bank account when he laid eyes upon the man responsible for fetching him here coming out of the Cowboy Saloon. Al Allison picked up his gait as he began crossing over.

"Damn, John, it's been a spell." He struck out an eager hand, which his brother grasped. "How's the family?"

"Fine . . . and anxious to come out here." He jabbed a thumb westward over his shoulder. "Those backgrounding Big Horns look right pretty, Al. Great place for a town. And coming in there is sure a lot of fine grazing land."

"Told you you'd like Buffalo. Me, I came into town with Jack Flagg."

"Sure, one of your partners. Admire meeting Flagg and the others."

"Come on, John, Flagg and Nate Champion are camped out at Zindel's."

He began trudging downstreet alongside his brother, a few years younger and not as solid through the shoulders, and where John Tisdale's sandy hair was thinning out, Al Allison's Stetson pressed down upon a full head of hair. It was while he was over east in the Badlands that he'd first received a letter from Al, and as his brother had left Texas under a cloud, to John Tisdale any news at all had come as a surprise. Stealing glances at Al as they walked, he couldn't help noticing how fancy a dresser his brother had become, and he seemed more sure of himself. Though from Al Allison came the slight stench of whiskey mingled with the scent of tobacco smoke.

"Maybe, Al, I should deposit some money in that bank before we get to drinking."

"Maybe," responded Al Allison, "John, and speaking of money, I . . . well, I spent most of what you sent." A mercurial smile appeared. "Needed some ready cash to buy a few head of cattle. Soon's the market picks up, though, I plan to sell some cattle and pay you back."

"I see," said John Tisdale. "I was counting on that money being here, Al. But I figure you knew what you were doing." He couldn't help remembering at the moment just how shiftless and uncaring his brother had been. But after all, hadn't he responded by staking Al to a share of the Hat outfit? "Okay, guess it does take money to run a ranch. Another thing, what about these newspaper stories . . ."

"Rustling," snorted Al Allison. "That's a lot of damn lies put out by the cattle kings . . . and that lying Ijams down at Cheyenne. The Hat brand is registered at the courthouse . . . and it isn't rustling so much as it's this crazy Maverick Law. Damnedest law ever passed. According to it, only the cattle kings are entitled to put their brand on mavericks. All these cattle kings are squatters anyway. Come in here early on and claimed the water holes. An' if you control the water . . ."

"Yup, man's gotta water his stock for sure."

Al Allison brought his brother into Zindel's and they were beelining for its long mahogany bar when Jack Flagg called out to them.

"And you must be John," went on Flagg as he dragged another chair over. "Nate Champion— and the sheriff just dropped by to warn us about Canton being in town."

Sheriff Red Angus had dropped in about ten minutes ago, and he greeted the newcomer with a cordial smile, then reclaimed his chair as Jack Flagg called out to a bartender that another bottle of whiskey be brought over. "Frank Canton," the sheriff said to Tisdale, "is a stock detective. Canton's got a place south of here. Reason I dropped by was to tell these boys about Joe Elliott being here too. Them together here in Buffalo is a cause for worry."

"Another thing is that Red beat out Canton for sheriff . . . an' ever since, Canton's been mad as hell."

"Don't worry," put in Nate Champion, "there won't be any trouble. At least not in town. If they muster up enough courage to try anything, it'll be out there . . . and knowing Canton and Joe Elliott, when a man's by his lonesome."

But all these men, and this included John Tisdale, would have forced a six-gun showdown had they known that the words just spoken by Nate Champion were almost identical in nature to those coming from stock association detective Joe Elliott. He was chummed up with Frank Canton at the Old Court saloon, just the pair of them in a back room, Elliott drinking more than he should, and Frank Canton, tight-lipped as ever, tapping a .45 slug on the nicked table top.

Joe Elliott had a thin, cruel slab of mouth below high cheekbones, and his eyes kept going from his table companion to the open window or door and back again. The window faced away from the passing storm cloud but rainwater splattered in to cool the small room. Even so, Elliott was sweating.

"So, Frank, it's up to you as to how the job is done. There are plenty of spots to set up an ambush. It'll be close work, which means you can use that shotgun you Texans seem to favor."

"So they want Champion dead."

"For starters."

The steely blue eyes of Frank Canton held to those of Elliott. Plaguing Johnson County, as both of them knew, were a lot of outlaws and rustlers driven out of Montana. This didn't include other longriders drifting along the infamous Outlaw Trail and into Hole-in-the-Wall. The difficulty facing Canton was of his trying to police an area as big as a couple of Eastern states and split up the middle by the Big Horns. He considered anyone blackballed by the association to be a rustler, even some of his rancher neighbors, as Canton's ranch lay about a dozen miles south of Buffalo and close in against the first low range of the mountains called the Horn.

"The Hat outfit will be next."

"That Jack Flagg is a damned thief all right. One thing, Frank, the association mustn't be involved in this. At least until we see which way the wind blows down in the Sweetwater Valley. They arrested those who hung Cattle Kate. And Major Wolcott sent Morrison down to Casper to more or less advise those ranchers."

"I know Albert Bothwell," Canton retorted as he brushed a fly away from his mustache. "He'll either buy off those witnesses to the hanging or kill 'em. And if they do drop the charges against those ranchers, it'll be a clear signal to the association that the law is on our side."

"There's Wolcott's death list."

"First there's Nate Champion . . . and Flagg . . . and a few others. Here's how we'll work it."

Five

The gutteral *ha-ya-ya-ya* of Sioux Indians
gyrating through one of their tribal dances greeted
James Haskins as he came out of the Hotel De
Wentworth. Striding under the alcove, he paused
to finger out his watch. It was eight-fifteen, with
the sun just clearing the buildings of Casper. He'd
arrived late yesterday afternoon on a Chicago &
Northwestern passenger train. His inquiries had
taken Haskins downstreet to the *Wyoming Derrick*, only to find the newspaper office closed for
the day. Then he'd found a hotel before making
the rounds of the saloons and dance halls. Most of
the bar talk had been about the ranchers involved
in the hanging of Cattle Kate and of how they'd
been arrested only to be released on their own
cognizance.

He took in the townspeople encircling the small
band of Sioux, feathered and with sweat glistening
on coppery skin, their shuffling moccasins stirring dust in a big empty lot just north of the hotel.
A dying remnant, he mused wistfully, of what this
land had once been. As for Casper, it was more of
an oil town than a place having to depend upon

53

the caprices of the rancher. Through here flowed the great river road, the North Platte, a watery magnet drawing in travelers, and Haskins had also found out to his immense pleasure, a river swarming with trout. Also through this tent town fast becoming a modest city passed the old historic trails—Bozeman, Oregon, the Pony Express, the Chisholm, and other cattle trails venturing up from Texas. The reporter from the *Chicago Gazette* had also learned that here men spoke out boldly, the talk being that James Averell and Cattle Kate hadn't been rustlers at all.

"Greed."

Another whiskey-soaked voice had rasped out in one of the many bars last night, "Just damned arrogance as those ranchers want it all."

It was evident to James Haskins folks hereabouts had little use for the cattle kings or for Cheyenne. But hard feelings were a poor substitute for steely-cold facts. The way a lot of other reporters had been doing it, this slurring over of facts just to send copy back East wasn't James Haskins's style. Back at Cheyenne it had been so easy to fall under the spell of the cattle kings' narrations about the rustlers. As for the truth about the hangings, he had it in mind to journey over to the Sweetwater Valley, even though he'd learned Westerners rarely opened up to strangers.

Hesitant about heading over to the newspaper office or seeking out a waking cup of coffee, he sent a lazy glance upstreet. A string of freight wagons came out of a side street and creaked by, and then beyond the wagons a face under a gray Stetson caused surprise to flicker into his eyes, and he murmured wonderingly:

"That's George Henderson—must have come in

on the same train." And the man accompanying Henderson, yes, one of those detectives working for the stockmen's association. They were here no doubt on orders from Major Wolcott. He supposed that Henderson would head back to the Sweetwater, but not before getting together with those ranchers who'd been released from jail and doing some celebrating. A callous breed, Haskins mused as Henderson and the other man went around a corner.

This set James into motion, to leave behind the hotel and the ha-yaying of the Sioux. The walk to the glass-fronted building occupied by the *Wyoming Derrick* served to get rid of some morning stiffness, with his passage through the open doorway noted by a few loafing on benches placed under the covering porch. A chair creaking brought Haskins over to an open door, where he thrust his shoulders in and inquired, "Mr. Cunningham?"

Without lifting his eyes, the bearded man seated behind the desk said caustically, "Sorry, got no time for carpetbaggers."

"Neither have I."

"Or idle prattling."

"Sir," James Haskins said insistently, "I came here hoping to find out more about the hangings . . . among other things. I'm Haskins . . . of the *Chicago Gazette.*"

"Very well," groused A. J. Cunningham as he tipped his hat back. Cynical eyes took in the Eastern attire, and somewhat reluctantly he pointed a grudging hand at a chair. "How long you been out here?"

"Long enough to know Cheyenne is trying to rule the roost."

"The association," he said glumly.

"I was there when George Henderson came in— this was shortly after the hangings. It was as if he already knew what had taken place, though Henderson did produce that telegram."

"He probably set the whole thing up," said editor Cunningham. "A lot of untruths have been set into print."

"Told mostly by Cheyenne."

"What was that name again?"

"Haskins, sir, James Haskins."

"Expect they call you Jim." Reaching over, he picked up the coffee pot and gurgled coffee into a cup, which he slid across the desk, and poured some more coffee into his. "Tastes only a mite better than horse droppings . . . but it fills the empty spots."

"Obliged."

"You picked that word up in some Cheyenne bawdy house."

"Close, Mr. Cunningham. And you're right about the coffee."

"I suppose you've heard about this coroner's jury being impaneled. An inquest will convene later this morning. Damned shame about it is that a couple of horse thiefs are on the jury. Anyway, they'll be questioning those who witnessed the hangings."

"Perhaps that's why George Henderson is here."

Grimacing his displeasure, Cunningham said, "I don't like the way this is shaping up. As first of all, those ranchers were turned loose before any testimony was aired. Which tells me they've put themselves above the law. They were let out yesterday. But some of them, Bothwell and two others, are still in town."

"I've heard stories about Bothwell—a hard man."

"An arrogant sonofabitch if ever there was one."

Sipping at the coffee, and his eyes narrowing thoughtfully, James Haskins said, "There's a possibility he might try to bribe those witnesses or even . . ."

"Or even, Haskins, is what worries me. Those ranchers feel they're in the right. Going to jail doesn't figure into their plans. They might do worse than try to bribe those witnesses."

"What can we do about it?"

"As newspapermen, certainly not print a lot of libelous statements. But just keep poking around until we find the truth or true intentions of these ranchers—then print it."

The Sioux dancers, after scrambling to pick up coin tossed their way, had returned to their camp eastward along the North Platte. Replacing this source of amusement was a trained dog act presided over by a man so thin he seemed to cast no shadow, the dogs being sent through their paces just beyond where the coroner's jury was still impaneled.

Although the editor of the *Wyoming Derrick* had escaped to a saloon to keep out of the rising heat of day, James Haskins chewed on an apple from where he waited out front of a grocery store and across from the Graham House. To his left under the porch a man perched on a barrel was regaling a couple of other cronies as to his sexual prowess while down in the Sandbar, Casper's infamous red-light district. And of George Henderson and the stock detective, there had been no sign, though someone had remarked that John Durbin, one of the ranchers involved in the hangings, was playing five-card stud over at the Crystal Saloon.

"I'd probably hang around too," James Haskins said inwardly, "if the testimony of those witnesses could send me to prison." His purpose for being here was to interview the men being questioned by the coroner's jury. But the heat was getting to him, and thirst drove him to seek a cooling drink of water. Those gathered closer to the hotel began scattering, and Haskins crossed the street only to learn that the coroner's jury had just been dismissed.

"Went out the back way," someone called out.

"What about the witnesses?"

A muleskinner turned to Haskins and said, "Probably heading out. Leastways that's what I'd be doing if I'd been forced to testify against them killing ranchers."

After a quick and appreciative nod, James Haskins began striding downstreet toward the Star livery stable. There were four witnesses—the Crowder boy and three men—one of whom he'd watched come out of the livery stable earlier this morning. He kept glancing at the business places to either side in an attempt to pick out Henderson or one of the ranchers, but the boardwalks were crowded. He came upon the livery stable just as Ralph Cole emerged with his bronc trailing behind.

"Excuse me, Mr. Cole, I wonder if I might have a word with you? Please"—he read the naked hesitancy in the cowhand's eyes—"I'm a reporter for the *Chicago Gazette*."

"Mister, I'm in one hell of a hurry." But Ralph Cole held there, staring warily at the intruder and beyond Haskins at the streets of Casper. He spun around on worn boot heels, thrust a boot into a stirrup, and pulled himself into the cherry-leather Texas saddle. That he was worried revealed itself in the way he held the reins so that his bronc began fighting the bit. He wasn't a tall man and he was small-boned. Sweat had worked through so that his light blue shirt clung to his chest and arms and stained his shaped and worn hat. At least a three-day stubble of brownish beard lay over his angular jawline and lower cheeks. Cole suddenly blurted out:

"You heard what happened?"

"That you named those responsible for hanging Cattle Kate."

"Yup, we sure as hell did."

"You knew her and James Averell."

"So I did."

"So the truth was that Averell and Cattle Kate were falsely accused of rustling: at least that's what I'm hearing."

"Mister, to me she'll always be Ella . . . just Ella Watson. Hell no, they weren't rustlers, Ella and Jim. It was just Bothwell wanting them out, damn his greedy hide."

"How does George Henderson figure in this?"

"He figures in it awright. Word is out Henderson was with them ranchers shortly a-fore they hit Ella's place. Then he shows up in Cheyenne claiming to have no knowledge of what happened."

"Yes, I was there when Henderson showed up. By the way, Mr. Cole, Henderson's in town— Henderson and an association detective."

Ralph Cole's eyes lidded over in fear, and he reined his horse away so abruptly that it brought James Haskins jumping backward to keep from being run-over. Cole disappeared around a side wall, the sound of his horse breaking into a gallop coming back to Haskins.

He stood there wondering, "Is Cole's fear of the ranchers justified?" Surely the ranchers wouldn't be so callously bold as to take out Cole or the other witnesses. But this was a hard land ruled by hard men. Which meant to him that Cole's fears were justified.

The gist of what would be in his next story started forming, but he felt just the few words of a frightened man weren't enough, that in fairness to those ranchers what he needed would be their viewpoint, of being arrested and of the coroner's jury returning a verdict that "the deceased came to their deaths by hanging" by six individuals who were named and along with this the addition of an alleged unknown man, whom Haskins knew had to be George Henderson. But again his reporter's ear told him not to be speculative over this but seek the truth, and he found himself passing along the street toward the Crystal Saloon.

Only he never got there as from an alleyway to intercept James Haskins stepped one of the Sweetwater witnesses. "I saw you talking to Ralph Cole," Frank Buchanan said quietly. "Expect you're a reporter."

Nodding, Haskins said, "And you're Mr. Buchanan."

Through a pensive smile Buchanan said, "Cole left rather hurriedly. Which I'll be doing before long. But there's a few things I want to get off my chest. And not here either but yonder in a backstreet saloon."

Along the way, this through some alleys and side streets, Haskins revealed his name and also his purpose for coming here. "But I had no idea you and the other witnesses were called here to testify."

Buchanan gave his response after they'd taken over a table in the Laramie Bar, a seedy place occupied mostly by oldtimers and its only attraction a back pool table. "We did testify, Mr. Haskins. To the effect that Ella and Jim were murdered. It was simply an execution ordered by Bothwell and backed up by the others. I . . . I tried to do what I could. But my sidearm against their rifles was no match." He refilled his stein from the cold pitcher of beer, Frank Buchanan being a tall and lean man with a pleasant face marred by sadness.

"Could this unknown man be George Henderson?"

"It is Henderson."

"I told Ralph Cole that Henderson was in town. Then Cole took off."

"Don't blame Cole for doing so as Henderson is a hard man. Manages the 71 Quarter Circle ranch. He's strictly an association man."

"Just who ordered the hangings?"

"Not the stockmen's association, Mr. Haskins. This was all Bothwell's doing."

"Do you feel that your life is in danger?"

"I know it is," came Frank Buchanan's bitter reply. Again that wry grin. "There's law of a sort out here. But when men take it into their own hands, they should be brought to task. I don't believe this will prove to be the case for those who strung up Ella and Jim. If they aren't brought to trial . . . if the charges against them are dropped . . . it'll be a signal to the stockmen's association that the rustlers of Wyoming are fair game."

"This is what I'm beginning to believe, Mr. Buchanan. If the charges are dropped? This could only mean the witnesses must be eliminated . . . somehow."

"Gunned down is how we phrase it out here, Mr. Haskins."

"You believe this'll happen?"

"Yup," Buchanan said calmly, with a wary glance toward the batwings and the windows to either side. "My only crime was being out there when it happened. And anyone wanting to homestead out here, it seems, or acquire himself a few cattle, is also branded a criminal. Sir, I'm about talked out."

"Is there anything I can do?"

"Just print the truth of what I've just told you in your newspaper, Mr. Haskins. But when you do, sir, keep watching your backside." He emptied what beer there remained in the pitcher into their steins. "You said you were heading up to Johnson County?"

"This is where all the rustlers seem to be located."

"A dangerous place for lawmen and newspaper reporters. Not so much because of the rustlers, Mr. Haskins, but mostly due to the stockmen's association having a lot of their men up thataway— especially that Frank Canton."

"The former sheriff of Johnson County?"

"Now working hand in glove with other stock detectives. You print unkind words about Canton he just might use that shotgun he favors."

"What about you, Frank, where are you heading from here?"

"Don't rightly know . . . or how far I'll get before something happens. I suppose you didn't know but that one of the witnesses, the Crowder boy, was taken in tow by one of those ranchers. The boy's been sickly; just might get a helluva lot sicker too. Yup"—there was a smile for the dubious glint in Haskins's eyes—"even yonkers aren't safe out here when it comes to Albert Bothwell."

It came to James Haskins then, that he was out here in a place of sudden violence, where men wore sidearms and used them, and that Buchanan's telling of the events in the Sweetwater was untarnished. He found himself bidding the cowhand good-bye, then Frank Buchanan slipped out the back door. He felt a sudden chill and hastily sought the batwings.

"How far will these ranchers go?"

As quickly as sunlight springing out from under a cloud shadow, the answer came to reporter James Haskins.

"Buchanan, Cole, the other witnesses, are going to be killed. Killed by the heavy hand of power and money . . . done in by greedy men."

Six

It took Ralph Cole a little over a day to work southward around Casper Mountain and down into more familiar country. Along the way he'd kept to dry washes and other low spots, just heading his bronc away from Casper and the man he knew would be coming after him. For he shared the fears of DeCorey and Frank Buchanan that they were doomed men as was the Crowder boy.

Going to Casper and testifying before that coroner's jury had taken its toll on Ralph Cole. Worrying about it had caused him to shed some pounds so that his shirt and leather coat hung more loosely. He should have grabbed a bite to eat before leaving, as he'd planned to do at a café fringing onto the edges of Casper, but the word from that meddling newspaperman had been that George Henderson was in town.

"But this is all Bothwell's fault," said Ralph Cole as he spurred his bronc onto higher ground. He felt the grime of trail dust kicked up by the steady southeasterly wind, and he muttered a tired oath as, in swinging out of the saddle, his right boot slipped off a crumbly rock to buckle his knees. His horse was too tired to sidestep away. Farther up in rocks being draped by twilight came the faint rattling of a sidewinder. Now the bronc tried pulling away but a hard jerk on the reins served to calm it down.

"Snakes and that damned Henderson—it just ain't my day."

Unstrapping his canteen from the saddle horn, he gulped down the warm, brackish water, and recorked the canteen while stabbing out a searching gaze northerly. He could still pick out traces of the Oregon Trail, and his gaze went from there to the lower sweep of prairie fringing away from this much-traveled roadway to the varying draws and coulees to either side as he figured Henderson would keep to shelter too. Earlier a stagecoach had rattled by, with Cole viewing it from concealment. If it had been heading south, he would have headed in and claimed a seat. Once some cowhands passing by a far piece from the trail had spotted Ralph Cole, who'd melted back into an arroyo as he'd been able to pick out Albert Bothwell's brand on the horses they were riding.

Cole was beginning to realize he should have broken farther to the east to come around the Laramies. But through here was the shortest way to the Rock Creek Station on the Union Pacific Railroad. There he could sell his horse and once aboard a westbound train leave Wyoming for good.

Now a weary Ralph Cole lifted himself into the saddle. He spurred to lower ground where deepening shadows pushed away sunlight. The temptation came to pass by Jim Averell's road ranch, thought it more likely the place would be shuttered down since nobody had laid claim to it.

66

Maybe Albert Bothwell would now that he'd murdered Averell.

Cole possessed an ability to see better'n most at night. So he kept to the saddle though clouds had moved in to blot out the stars. Some of his worry over being followed passed away as the night pressed closer around him. The cooling air caused his bronc to step a little livelier, though its rider knew he wasn't about to push on too much longer.

At first he wasn't sure, thinking it was just more lightning, but now he could make out the darker stands of trees lining the Sweetwater and the campfire. It could be most anybody, was Cole's musings as he angled that way while taking in a little rein. Habit made him touch the butt of his .38 Colt. The ground was rough, forcing him to ride around low spots and clumps of sagebrush, then he realized the camp was out in the open alongside the river, the gear in one of the wagons belonging to surveyors. He rode in more boldly as someone called out in a friendly tone of voice:

"Evening, stranger."

The flames of the large fire reaching out to him, Ralph Cole reined up within its beckoning light and for the benefit of the three men allowed a smile to show. "That Arbuckles sure smells tempting."

"It does at that," remarked one of the men, who said he was Aaron Delevan and out here surveying for a land company. "Our vittles are still hot, Mr. Cole. You just passing by?"

"More or less. Just might bedroll down under those trees if you gents don't mind."

"Our pleasure. You rode in from the north?"

"Left Casper some time ago," he volunteered as a tin cup was passed to him, and hunkering down, a plate heavy with beans and meat and greens. From there on, Cole's responses to the questions tossed at him by the surveyors were guarded.

Ralph Cole stole out of camp well before daylight could lift the screening night shadows. Southward he pressed, making better time during the day as his belly had been filled and his bronc rested. He felt a lot better about his chances of reaching Rock Creek Station, certain he'd gained ground on George Henderson.

"Man's got Eastern roots," he said jestingly. "So's he can't set the saddle long as me . . . or other genuine cowpokes."

Back at Casper they had split up, stockmen's association detective Ben Morrison taking out after Frank Buchanan, and George Henderson taking it upon himself to strike the backtrail of Ralph Cole. But unlike Cole, who he reckoned had a few hours' start on him, Henderson, the manager of the 71 Quarter Circle Ranch, had come south on the main road. Before leaving Casper, he had reassured Albert Bothwell that Cole would never reach the Rock Creek Station.

"How can you be sure Cole's beelining there?"

"The man's riding scared, Albert. He's not packing any food. So I figure he'll stop someplace along the way."

"I just want Cole dead."

"Albert, you'll never see Cole again."

"De Corey, who's going after DeCorey?"

"That I'll leave in your hands. Remember, DeCorey can run, Albert, but he can't hide."

So armed and laden down with provisions bulging out his saddlebags, George Henderson had taken up the chase. One of his precautions had been to pack along a field glass. The rifle, a Winchester, had a scope attached to it. On his second day out of Casper, Henderson was enjoying himself. He knew all about chasing men, having been a Pinkerton and once a member of the coal and iron police back in Pennsylvania. To this end he had been forced to kill a couple of men.

Late last night he'd spotted the glowing camp-fire farther to the east, had kept to the saddle, though, and at the moment it was his opinion that he'd gotten ahead of the fleeing Ralph Cole. Though his eyes were red-rimmed and squinty from lack of sleep, the whiskey he'd packed along had helped him shrug off this discomfort. What he was seeking now as he studied Ferris Mountain just to the south was a place to set up an ambush. He discarded the thought that Cole would swing west toward South Pass City. That would bring Cole farther away from the main line of the Union Pacific. No, Henderson mused firmly, Cole was heading for Rock Creek Station.

He came to a place called Whiskey Gap, a gap between dolomite rocks soaring upward around eight hundred feet, and deeper into the gap, he rode alongside Whiskey Creek. Through the gap passed a country road which would take a traveler down to Rawlins. Cutting away from the road, Henderson soon found a height to his liking, an outcropping of rock jutting out to give anyone up there an uncluttered view of the road and creek below and the approaches into the gap. In here were hunks of trees that had died, wood that would come in handy for what George Henderson had in mind. But first he had to find out if Ralph Cole was on the way.

Tying his horse in underbrush, he left it grazing as he scaled the height armed only with his holstered sidearm, the field glass, and to sate his thirst, a bottle of whiskey. Settled in on the outcropping, he scanned the northern approaches to Whiskey Gap from time to time, while sipping at a drink of the same name. The birds he had first scared up upon his arrival soon quieted down, and suddenly he was catnapping. Sometime later an acquired sense that someone was approaching jerked Henderson's eyes open. When the field glass found his right eye, George Henderson spotted the man he was chasing.

"About four to five miles out and coming in warily," was his happy response. Leaving the whiskey bottle but taking along his field glass, he made his way down to the bay to claim his Winchester.

Back on the rocky height, George Henderson fussed with the scope and workings of his rifle. It wouldn't do to just kill Ralph Cole and then bury the body, especially here where passersby often stopped. To this end the lackey for the cattle kings had something else in mind, the thought of which brought a pleased smile tugging at his wide mouth. And then through the scope he could make out every detail of Cole's face, the anxious shifting of the eyes and spittle on the stubbled face when the waddy hawked out tobacco juice. He let the rider come into the gap, let Cole veer under a screening pine as he held there to get his bearings and to determine if danger lurked close at hand.

From the man's head he lowered the scope on his Winchester until the barrel was sighting in on Ralph Cole's midriff, for it wasn't the intention of Henderson to have Cole die so quickly. And with this in mind, he waited until his prey had dismounted and was letting his horse drink at the stream, while Ralph Cole kneeled down to refill his canteen.

In the close confinements of the gap, the barking of George Henderson's Winchester sounded louder than normal, the canyon walls ripping back the reverberating bark again and again even as the leaden slug ripped into Ralph Cole's lower back. The impact of the slug knocked Cole forward into the creek as his bronc bolted across it. His agonizing scream of fear and pain came up to George Henderson rising from his sitting position on the outcropping. From this height he could see that Cole could barely cling to a clump of brush in an attempt to keep his head above water, and hurriedly now Henderson clambered down. He paused long enough by his horse to leather the Winchester and then he brought the horse across the roadway and to the creek.

Groundhitching the reins, he ambled down the creek bank, swept Cole's hat away and fastened his hand in the man's thinning and greasy head of hair. He managed to pull Cole onto the bank, while Cole tried to say something before he went limp.

It was the awful heat more than the flickering flames that aroused Ralph Cole. He was still in shock over what had happened, that and the terrible pain eating at his lower back. But there was enough awareness for the unlucky Ralph Cole to suddenly comprehend he'd been staked out, and that dry hunks of wood were stacked around him to form sort of an imprisoning cage. And that he could barely make out the vague form of the man who'd shot him peering down a short distance away, and this due to the heavy film of smoke issuing from the burning wood.

"What the—"

"Cole, it is your time to pay for your sins."

"No? No? Noooo!"

Only now did Ralph Cole realize the other pain he was feeling came not from the bullet wound but the fire eating eagerly at his pinioned frame, and there was also a stench of burning flesh.

"You shouldn't have spilled your guts to that coroner's jury, Cole."

"The truth—I told the truth!"

At that moment flames began consuming Ralph Cole's hair and the agony of what was happening brought a terrible scream ripping out of his suffering body. That scream went on and on and on until a final spasm wracked his body and he died, while through all of this George Henderson kept sipping at his whiskey and smiling.

After the flames had gone out, all that was left for George Henderson to do was bury the few bones that remained. Earlier he had ridden out to rope Cole's horse, and in leaving Whiskey Gap, he brought it along. He found the deep recesses of another canyon, there to discard the saddle and other rigging, and here he turned the horse loose. Then he set out for the ranch he managed.

"I expect by now Morrison has taken care of Frank Buchanan. But even if he hasn't, you can rest assured the other witnesses won't be around much longer. Then what happens to other rustlers is up to Major Wolcott and the stockmen's association."

The offices of the Wyoming Stock Grower's Association were closing for the day when one of its employees arrived. And without preamble, Major Frank Wolcott brought association detective Ben Morrison into his office and made certain the door was closed. It was Morrison speaking out first, his words bringing an unaccustomed smile to Wolcott's squarish face.

"So one of them, Cole, is dead."

"Frank Buchanan got away from me. But we'll hound him down if he's still in Wyoming. Here's another piece of good news, Major Wolcott." This was Morrison's telling the major that the Crowder boy had passed away. According to a doctor, it was from Bright's disease. Ben Morrison didn't have to add that the boy had lingered on for some weeks, and finally succumbed to a slow poison administered by his protectors, the cattlemen who'd taken him in.

"Well," Wolcott said in his rapid-fire voice, "this is all well and good. But the fact remains Bothwell and the others must stand trial."

"Not if the other witnesses are taken care of."

"Ben, from here on in, stay away from Casper. For now we'll just lay back and see how it goes up there. What I'm saying is that I don't want the association tainted by further involvement with Bothwell. Yes, yes, Bothwell's a dues-paying member . . . but nevertheless a hothead. Our immediate problem is up in Johnson County."

"The association still thinking of getting some men together and heading up there?"

"That, Ben, is still in the fire. At the moment Joe Elliott's up there. I want you to get word to Joe and, of course, Frank Canton, that Nate Champion has to go."

"Wouldn't it be simpler to send a telegram up there?"

"Nope," Wolcott said curtly. "Because I don't

want word getting out about this. That damned Champion is the leader of a bunch of rustlers. Kill him and things might change. Now, Ben, that will be all as I'm taking my wife to Friday night services at our church. I truly enjoy our choir; such joy their singing brings to my soul."

"That might suit you, Major Wolcott, but I'm off to find my joy at a few saloons." Over his shoulder Ben Morrison added, "I'll catch the morning train."

Seven

Some ten years back Nate Champion had left Williamson County, Texas, the cradle of cowboys, to help bring a trail herd up the Chisholm Trail. Taking a liking to rawboned territorial Wyoming, he soon found work at the EK Ranch, and then later accepted a job as wagon boss for the Bar C, both of these cattle spreads being located in northern Wyoming and looking onto the Big Horns. Later on, Nate Champion went to work for the EK again, but through some misunderstanding Nate and two other cowboys were fired.

As for the makeup of Nate Champion, he was laconic and soft-spoken, but he would stand up to anybody. Possessed of a stocky frame and steely blue-gray eyes, he had earned a reputation as being fast with a gun. A smile always seemed to grace Nate's square, dark-complexioned face topped by unruly sandy hair, as though he was always looking to pull a joke on someone. This was probably the reason the small ranchers, such as he had become, the sheepmen, and the homesteaders looked up to him. And something that the cattle kings had taken note of. But the fear of the big ranchers was that Nate Champion in the years he'd worked for them knew a lot of their secrets, and it was this more than anything which had caused these men and the stockmen's association to place Champion on their blacklist.

Nate Champion was no different from other cowhands let go by the big ranchers during these lean years in that he wanted to start a ranch of his own. With this in mind he had gone up to nearby Buffalo and gotten his brand registered. And like others taking this step, Nate Champion had simply ignored the biting insult of the Maverick Law, either by buying a few head of cattle or, when finding one without a brand, slapping his brand on it.

A couple of years ago Nate Champion, in looking about for summer grazing land, decided to bring his herd to a large parcel of land known thereabouts as the Bar C pasture. This was actually the red-walled valley of Buffalo Creek, the narrow valley running about thirty miles north to south, guarded westward by the Big Horns and opposite a red-rock wall which along its entire length had only four narrow openings. The valley was about a hundred thousand acres of grazing land having been left vacant when the Bar C ranch went under. But when Champion got his small herd over there, it was to discover that cattle king Robert Tisdale had brought in around two thousand head of cattle. Undismayed by this, Champion simply turned his herd loose, as he figured there was enough grass and water for both herds. The upshoot of this was that an angry rancher Tisdale rounded his cattle up and a lot of Champion's and found other grazing land.

At the moment Nate Champion was thinking

76

about this as he began taking supplies off the pack horse and carrying them into a cabin he'd rented. Afterward, his musings went, he had ridden in on Tisdale's roundup on the South Fork. With Nate were a few friends, and they'd proceeded to cull out a bunch of calves, which he believed were rightfully his, and then started their own branding fire. The hands working for cattle king Robert Tisdale had simply watched from a safe distance as they were drawing pay as working cowhands, not as hired guns. This incident more than anything led to Champion's being called a rustler.

"Rustler, hell," he muttered, "I was just going after cattle legally belonging to me."

The plans of Nate Champion were to winter here in the old Hall cabin. It lay way up on the headwaters of the Middle Fork, about a mile from the old Bar C headquarters. Situated in a pocket of a valley, barely a half-mile long, there were thick stands of trees and brush and sheer red sandstone walls guarding the cabin, which one could reach only by passing along a trail hidden in a narrow draw. He wouldn't winter alone but share the two-room cabin with cowhand Ross Gilbertson, who'd taken off for Buffalo a couple of days ago. Though he expected Gilbertson to turn up most anytime, Champion enjoyed the solitude of the valley.

Another reason Nate Champion wanted to be alone had to do with a young woman residing in Buffalo. It had all come about so unexpectedly, him showing up at a Saturday night dance going on at the Occidental Hotel, to get a glimpse of Corrie Middleton. At first he'd gotten the impression this flaxen-haired woman of about twenty had bold eyes, then in moving out of the shadowed doorway to bunch in with others lining

77

the hardwood floor, he realized it was just Corrie's way. A quiet inquiry revealed the Middleton's had moved here from Denver, with William Middleton opening a haberdashery. Somehow Nate found himself cutting in to dance with her, and that was how it started.

Spring passed into a summer they began calling a weather breeder, as every day seemed to be cloudless and the nights all silvery and starlighted. There were times when Nate had just saddled up and headed into town to see Corrie. Then, and he could recall the painful moment, Corrie's father had told Nate Champion that he didn't want any rustler sparking his daughter. So he'd simply climbed back into the saddle and left. Thereafter to avoid Corrie Middleton, though once she'd intercepted him on the road heading south out of Buffalo.

"Is it true what they say about you, Nate Champion?"

"What is the truth in these parts, Corrie? Those stories spread by the big ranchers? Sure, there are a lot of thieves around these parts, and rustlers, I reckon."

"You do hang out with Jack Flagg . . ."

"Jack's outspoken, for certain."

"And said to be a rustler. Is that true?"

"Corrie, this is the gospel of it. Anybody bucking the big outfits is being branded a thief. As for me, I've got around two hundred head . . . and not a rustled cow in the bunch. But they say differently, the big outfits. I—I was gonna ask you . . ."

"Go on?"

"But that'll spill the beans as to how I feel about you, Corrie. Nope, when things simmer down, maybe it'll be a heap different. Now it's hard bucking your pa, and a lot of lying tongues.''

He could still remember so vividly that flicker of pain and wonderment which had radiated out of Corrie Middleton's eyes, and of how he had turned his back on her and simply ridden away. Now he couldn't help feeling that maybe she was too young for him, and perhaps not even suited to ranch life. But she was a looker, and in Nate Champion still lingered the deep feelings he had for her. Let it rest, he told himself, and with that Nate brought the packhorse over to the lonely pole corral. Removing the pack, he turned the horse into the corral and went into the cabin to build up the fire in the cast iron stove.

When he emerged from the cabin, it was barely coming onto noon, the wind moaning above the redstone walls, and the depths of this small valley filled with the traces of autumn, the leafs turning on trees and the air cool as a pitcher of buttermilk just lifted out of a cistern. Earlier today he'd taken stock of their food staples, and knew what they had wouldn't last more'n a couple of months at most. They could make do for now, but oftentimes early winter storms would strike without warning, blocking the narrow passage in here or many of the roads radiating toward Buffalo.

In the morning the passage of Nate Champion out of the valley was duly noticed by a puma crouched on a faraway ledge. He'd brought along the packhorse. Along the way he anticipated running into Ross Gilbertson, though he knew Ross wasn't dependable when it came time to leave the bright lights and gaming dens of Buffalo or any cow town.

But what Nate Champion hadn't taken into consideration, and which caused a worried frown to crease his forehead, was the sight of a lone rider coming his way on the narrow patch of trail running northeasterly. "Mike Shonsey isn't out here just to pass the time of day."

After quitting the CY, Nate Champion recalled, Shonsey had managed to wrangle a job as bossman of the Frontier Cattle Company, which was made up of the EK and NH outfits and what was left of the old Bar C. Once he'd ridden over there to tell Shonsey that some of his cattle had accidentally gotten into Shonsey's herd and that he would like to get them out. This request was refused by Shonsey, but after Nate had taken his departure, Mike Shonsey had cut them out and run the cattle off. Later on he'd encountered Shonsey in town and laid a few harsh words upon the ranch foreman. But of a more worrisome nature was Shonsey's trying to butter up to the men blackballed by the association. Since Shonsey was thick with ranch detective Canton and the cattle kings, Nate had come to the conclusion that Mike Shonsey was merely spying on him and other small ranchers, and the thought rankled him as Shonsey waved casually upon reining up.

"You heading out someplace, Nate?"

"No," he said sarcastically, "I'm just exercising my packhorse. You lost?"

The smile of Shonsey's was still there, and he said casually, "You've got some horses I'd like to buy. Those geldings of yours, Nate."

"They're fine animals, awright."

"Where's Gilbertson—sleeping off a drunk?"

"I thought you came here to do some hoss trading."

Hurriedly Mike Shonsey replied, "I'll give you a fair price for them geldings."

"Shonsey, they're for sale, but not to you." He reined his horses out. A couple of miles downtrail a look back revealed Shonsey coming Nate's way, and Nate Champion muttered caustically, "About as subtle as a burr under a saddle blanket."

Just when a cooling wind sent a tumbleweed whipping out in front of Nate's bronc, he touched upon the main road passing northward toward Buffalo. To his left rose the Big Horns, and he took them in, his sweeping glance encompassing the jagged peaks strung together under stark white clouds. As he rode over an undulation, there appeared below on the road a man nursing along a limping horse. "Stranger to these parts," was Nate's comment as he closed in.

Four days ago James Haskins had left Casper on a grain-fed horse. What he'd encountered along the way had been cold nights spent shivering in his bedroll, the yowling of coyotes causing him to stay awake for long spells of time, and both Haskins and the black gelding thinning out. A day ago he'd run out of food, had managed to sustain himself on what was left of his Arbuckles. Once he'd encountered five cowhands drifting past him toward Kaycee. Cold eyes had taken in what Haskins had on even as their gunhands stayed close to holstered weapons. In passing they left behind pitying glances for the condition of Haskins and his horse, and never uttered a word or left so much as a good-bye wave.

Aware now of someone coming in from behind, James Haskins twisted wearily in the saddle, to be greeted by a smile from the stranger trailing the backhorse. "Hello, er, howdy, mister."

"Howdy yourself, stranger. That horse still alive?"

"I guess so." His smile matched Nate Champion's.

"No sense crippling that hoss further, as it's

thrown a shoe. Guess you'd better climb aboard my packhorse. Now just what in tarnation is a greenhorn such as yourself doing out here by his lonesome?"

"Heading for Buffalo. How far north is it?"

"Up yonder." Nate Champion watched through amused eyes as Haskins managed to wedge himself a seat on the packhorse, and then he passed to his new companion the reins of the other horse. "It should make it without too much trouble." He revealed his name, and that he was a rancher heading in to Buffalo to buy supplies.

"I'm James Haskins, a reporter."

"In that getup you could be an undertaker. From where, Haskins?"

"Out of Chicago . . . the *Chicago Gazette.*"

"Heard of Chicago but not that particular newspaper. Must not have much of a circulation." Champion got into the saddle, and then he tossed the reins of the packhorse to Haskins.

They rode alongside one another, exchanging small talk, when suddenly James Haskins exclaimed, "Seems to me your name was mentioned in some newspapers . . ."

"Could be" Nate smiled—"as they call me a rustler."

"I—I'm sorry," he stammered.

"Don't be, as you ain't the one accusing me of these things. One reason I don't read newspapers no more—just a pack of lies."

As they rode on, it suddenly came to James Haskins that his trail companion had a pleasant disposition, that Nate Champion didn't seem to have the earmarks of an outlaw. Then a question thrown at him by Champion brought this stammering response,

"No, Mr. Champion, I don't print all of what

82

Cheyenne tells me. That place is awful one-sided, it seems. On the one hand, there was a Cheyenne newspaper lauding the town of Buffalo—next I read where everyone up here is involved in this rustling."

"Not everyone, Mr. Haskins," said Champion from where he rode alongside the reporter from Chicago. "But up here you know who your friends are . . . and your enemies."

For James Haskins the cow town of Buffalo shadowed by the snowcapped peaks of the Big Horns turned out to be a pleasant interlude after his perilous journey up from Casper. He'd told Champion about running into those cowhands, which provoked from Champion an amused laugh and this comment:

"Maybe those boys figured you for a tax collector. If you're heeled, Mr. Haskins, I figure your first move is to buy some suitable clothing."

"This outfit is trailworn for sure," said James Haskins as he reined after Champion following the road twisting to the right and downward. To Haskins the town seemed more spacious than Casper, as Buffalo had brick buildings pushing onto a narrow main street and any number of pool halls, saloons, and mercantile stores. Lounging out in front of the Old Court Saloon were four soldiers, which reminded James Haskins that close at hand lay Fort McKinney. Their laughter accompanied Champion's grin as they took in the Easterner reining along the packhorse, and with one of the soldiers calling out:

"Hey, Nate, did you bag that greenhorn up in the Big Horns?"

"Just about. This here's"—doffing his hat, he

gestured toward Haskins—"a Jim Dandy reporter from Chicago." And more quietly he said to Haskins, "They'll find out soon enough what you're here for. Yonder's the Occidental; best hotel in Wyoming." He led the way across the narrow bridge spanning Clear Creek and veered over to rein up in front of one of the wide doors opening onto the Occidental taking up most of a long block.

"I'd better take care of my horse first," said Haskins upon coming off the packhorse.

"Reckon I'd better tend to that," put in Champion. "Just grab your saddlebags and head in to get a room and a hot bath. 'Cause I wouldn't want you expiring on me as you look awful peaked. Then I'd have to pack you on that hoss again and cart you over to the undertaker's."

Hefting his saddlebags, he left a tired smile for Champion and sought the cooler sanctuary of the hotel lobby. Within minutes he'd been escorted up to a second-story room, and shortly after that James Haskins was settling into a bathtub filled with steaming hot water. He realized that running into Nate Champion had been a stroke of luck, and also that he hadn't asked where Champion was going to take his horse. But then the soothing effects of the hot water on trail-weary muscles took over and he simply closed his eyes and let sleep take over. What roused him was a pail of cold water coming down to splash over his head, and he popped his eyes open as someone said loudly:

"I've got others waiting to use that bathtub, mister. And lucky thing I came along just now, or you just might have drowned. Gents like you shouldn't drink so much."

Haskins shrugged apologetically as the attendant slammed the door in leaving, and drying himself, he found his room and some wrinkled but clean clothing he'd rescued from his saddlebags. From the window he had a clearer view of this cow town spreading north to south and a few foothills farther to the east. It seemed peaceful enough, he mused, meaning since his arrival a couple of hours ago there hadn't been the sound of gunfire, as a lot of newspaper accounts had led him to believe. To the rumbling of an empty stomach he found the staircase and the dining room, where a few people were partaking of a midafternoon coffee break.

A waitress with an engaging smile brought him to a table, and he said, "Whatever you have."

"Mister, you or anybody else can't eat all of what's on our menu."

"Okay, something that won't take too long." And at her suggestion he took the beef stew and lemonade to chase it down.

As James Haskins surveyed the interior of this spacious hotel, he was beginning to realize that what had been written about the Occidental had only scratched the surface, for about the hotel was an elegance of design, and with a framed picture on the wall telling of the Occidental having sixty rooms, a large billiard hall, numerous sample rooms and a ballroom, a connecting livery stable. No rustler, was his silent comment, could ever construct such a place.

"Pardon me . . ."

Startled by the sound of her voice, he swung his head to the left to gaze up at the smiling face of a young woman, and he stammered, "Oh, I—I wasn't expecting anyone?"

"I saw you ride in with Nate."

"Nate Champion, yes." Awkwardly he pushed to his feet.

"I'm Corrie Middleton; a friend of Nate's. And

you're Mr. Haskins. I peeked at the register."

"Yes," he said upon taking in the oval face and dancing blue eyes, "James Haskins. Nate Champion more or less rescued me out there." He told her about his horse throwing a shoe. "I . . . please, have a chair . . . I mean, sit down." He could feel his cheeks tingling as Corrie Middleton eased onto a chair and ruffled out her skirts.

"I shouldn't say this, Mr. Haskins, but your clothes could certainly stand an iron."

"They are kind of wrinkled at that."

"Did Nate say anything about me?"

"About you? I—not to me."

"I suppose it really isn't important." She smiled through a brief moment of laughter. "I couldn't help noticing you coming in on that packhorse."

At that moment James Haskins decided he liked this laughing young woman, and a smile appeared. It was all too obvious that Corrie Middleton had a special interest in rancher Champion; this brought a tinge of envy.

"This Buffalo," he ventured, "is an interesting town."

"My father thought so. That's the reason he moved here from Denver, and to open a haberdashery shop. But mostly he sells Western clothing and such things."

"Which reminds me, Miss Middleton. Champion suggested I get rid of these clothes. Ah, perhaps you could tell me how to find the newspaper office?"

"You'll find it, as Buffalo isn't that big." She sprang up and added, "I'm sorry I bothered you about Nate. It's just . . . good-bye, Mr. Haskins."

With Corrie Middleton's departure his food arrived, to have James Haskins discover his plate was more than heaped with beef stew, and that it was delicious and warming to the stomach. While lingering were fragmented thoughts of the brief encounter with Corrie Middleton. Which brought him to the sudden conclusion that perhaps he might enjoy this cow town of Buffalo.

Upon leaving the dining room, he paused to obtain some writing material from the desk clerk, and brought this and a few fresh ideas up to his room. Making himself comfortable at a desk by the open window letting in balmy mountainous air, he brought the quilled pen scrawling across the yellowed sheet of paper. This new story for the *Chicago Gazette* would be all about his unexpected encounter with a man many considered a rustler, Nate Champion, and with a few afterthoughts thrown in about Buffalo.

"Perhaps I could even mention running into Corrie Middleton." At the moment he couldn't get the fathomless blue of her eyes out of his mind, or that bubbling laughter. She was no rustler, nor were the other people he'd seen thronging the streets.

"There's a story up here. Just hope I can figure all of it out."

Then his reporter's training took over and he bent to the task of placing his thoughts on paper.

Eight

By the end of the week everyone in Buffalo knew that a newspaperman from Chicago was in their midst. Buffalo's two newspapers, the *Bulletin* and the *Echo*, had competed in printing brief stories about James Haskins. Despite this, however, a lot of townspeople felt young Haskins could be a tool of the stockmen's association.

"I can't blame them," said James Haskins as he brought the surrey closer to the orderly buildings of Fort McKinney. Pulling up under an elm tree, he felt the touch of Corrie Middleton's hand.

"It's the way things are, Jim. It'll take some time for these people to open up to you."

"We seem to be running out of time up here," came his sobering remark. What had prompted this statement from Haskins was the startling news that all charges had been dropped against the ranchers involved in hanging Cattle Kate. He had heard that two of the witnesses to the hanging were dead, and this latest development could only mean that the others had suffered the same fate. The same newspaper had told of how the association had so callously named Albert Bothwell to be on its executive committee. It was James Haskins's fear that if the cattle kings could take the law into their hands and not be brought to task for it, they would do so again and again. Bloody times were coming for Johnson County.

"I'm glad your newspaper sent some of its latest issues out here. You know, you're a very good writer."

"Why, thank you, Corrie. I've tried to be fair in my assessment of what's been happening out here. That Buffalo is a town facing a difficult situation."

"One other thing, James Haskins. You keep a wary eye out for Frank Canton and his associates."

"I've only seen the man that one time. But yes, Corrie, perhaps my stories are slanted in favor of men like Nate Champion, and possibly Jack Flagg. If they were truly rustlers, surely they couldn't get their brands registered at the courthouse."

"You like Nate."

"He befriended me, Corrie. Nate's a hard man not to like. And what about you . . ."

"Jim, I just don't know," she said pensively as he swung the carriage around to begin the mile or so journey back into town. "Are you still planning on going to the town meeting tonight?"

About twenty minutes before the meeting was to begin at Buffalo's town hall, James Haskins strolled out of the Germania House Restaurant & Beer Depot, a place he'd started to frequent, and went upstreet. He couldn't help thinking of Corrie, that it had been her asking him to go for that buggy ride. Now she'd invited him over for supper tomorrow night. How he felt about Corrie Middleton hadn't firmed up in his mind, but there was little doubt that he enjoyed being around this pretentious and beautiful young woman. Along with Nate Champion, there were several local men vying to become her steady beau. Perhaps, he mused, she'd asked him over only because it was the Western way.

He took in the tidy buildings jutting to either side, with names such as C. P. Organ & Company, Webster & Platt's, Billy Hunt's, and the Minnie Ha-ha printed on showcase windows and signs. This street, he'd learned, was built on what had once been a trail that curved down a slight hill, to ford Clear Creek and angle up the grade on the other side. Ahead of him was located a large log building with a false front bearing the proclamation that its owner, a Scotsman named Bobby Foote, was a dealer in general merchandise. There was a second story, the sides of which had dormer windows. On the south side of the store a veranda had been added for the accommodation of the clientele. Bobby Foote had been about the first merchant to extend a welcoming hand.

Haskins was passing by the Scotsman's store when its owner chanced to come outside.

"Evening, Mr. Foote," Haskins greeted him. "I trust you're going to the meeting."

"That I am," Foote responded in his thick Scottish brogue. The white beard nearly touched the beltline of Bobby Foote's tailored pants. Somewhere in his travels the dapper little man had acquired a quadroon named Amanda as his wife. But Amanda Foote was accepted socially out here, and she ran her own business just across the street, a dry goods and millinery store. Foote had been shrewd enough to place his store at the intersection where the road from Fort McKinney came into town. And as Haskins had also learned, Bobby Foote was in the thick of community activities.

"Mr. Haskins, I read with great interest your story in the *Chicago Gazette*. It seems you weren't buffaloed by those cattle kings down in Cheyenne."

"All I'm looking for, sir, is the truth."

"Which might never come out," replied Foote as they began angling across the street. "What's happening out here is not just the issue of rustling. Sometimes it is the pitting of brother against brother. Or a wife, probably the daughter of a rancher, having her husband's name placed on the association's black list. My customers, Mr. Haskins, are the soldiers, drifters and what have you, the ranchers. As a merchant here, I must tread that fine line . . . and often, sir, I stumble."

"What about this feud between the sheriff and Frank Canton . . ."

"Canton's . . . well, Canton—arrogant and aloof. Canton smolders because Red Angus, a man who has lived in a saloon and a house of prostitution all of his life, was elected to the office of sheriff. Mark my words, Canton's nursing his wrath as he wanted that job."

The small packet sent from Cheyenne had arrived a couple of days ago. Upon opening it, Frank Canton took in Major Frank Wolcott's bold handwriting on the one-page letter, then riffled through the newspaper clippings which he'd also found in the packet. With him at the time had been

Ben Morrison and Joe Elliott, and cowman Mike Shonsey, who'd slunk up the back staircase then gained access to Elliott's room at a local boarding-house.

"Wolcott thinks we should do something about this meddling reporter, Haskins. Here, read these articles." Canton tossed the clippings onto the bed, where the others reached for them.

"According to this one," said Ben Morrison, "Haskins isn't at all certain Champion is a rustler. Or Flagg, for that matter. This is poisonous stuff, Frank."

"One more killing won't make much difference," said Joe Elliott.

"That reporter went to the meeting," volunteered Shonsey as he brought the whiskey bottle to his lips.

"Haskins isn't the one we have to worry about," Frank Canton said in that cold way of his. "Mike, you scouted out that cabin of Champion's . . ."

"Only one way in, Frank. So Nate and Gilbertson won't be able to get away."

"Good," nodded Canton. "As for Wolcott, and his damned letter, I don't see any need in doing away with Haskins. But some knuckles rattling against his skull should make that damned reporter realize he's backing the wrong side."

"I'll do it," Elliott said eagerly. "Ben, you want in on this?"

"Might's well as there isn't much happening in this town. Where's he staying, the Occidental?"

Nodding as the whiskey bottle was handed to him, Joe Elliott said, "We'll get him when he clears that meeting hall."

* * *

Under the impression this was just going to be a regular town meeting, James Haskins, upon arriving there, had been surprised to see that the large hall was packed, not only with townspeople, but virtually every person east of the Big Horns, although Champion and Ross Gilbertson had decided not to make the fifty-mile trip to town.

One of the first problems under discussion had to do with the recent stock-seizure move. Haskins listened spellbound as small ranchers described how their cattle had been seized upon arriving at the stockyards in Omaha. Their cattle had been sold, with the money being sent to the Wyoming Stock Growers' Association office at Cheyenne. More grievances came to light—that of the big outfits moving their large herds through the countryside, to carelessly knock down fences and trample garden plots, and of how the big herds collected the cattle of small owners in passing.

Then, as James Haskins sat there taking notes, a motion was made and promptly approved to form their own stockmen's association.

Seated next to Haskins was Bobby Foote, who stated plainly, "This'll bring the wrath of Cheyenne onto Johnson County for sure."

When the meeting finally broke up, Foote went over to discuss some business matters with other merchants, and James Haskins shouldered with others out the front door. On the way back to the Occidental, he detoured over to the Senate Saloon for a pondering glass of beer. The gist of the meeting had given him a clearer understanding of the problems of the small ranchers. But he also reflected on a chance conversation he'd had last week with the owner of the 4H Ranch, W. H. Holland. Holland's ranch lay a few miles east of

Buffalo, and the rancher, though aligned with the stockmen's association out of Cheyenne, had a lot of friends up here. It was from Holland he learned that a lot of the so-called cattle kings didn't approve of the methods being employed by Major Wolcott or the present secretary down in Cheyenne, H. B. Ijams. But what they loathed most was the infamous Maverick Law and all the trouble this law had caused. Wyoming, James Haskins was beginning to realize, had brought into being something that could destroy it.

Knowing that he wanted to place all of this on paper, he left without finishing his drink, to be one of those thronging the boardwalks. He got as far as the bridge passing over Clear Creek when a shove in his back by an insistent hand caused him to stumble toward an alleyway.

"Don't be foolish, Haskins," said the man behind him. "I just want to talk."

Another shove by Ben Morrison spilled Haskins farther into the alley, and then he glimpsed the other man up by some trash barrels. "Yeah, I've seen you before . . . yeah, at Casper."

Before he even had time to think about it, Joe Elliott's fist came loping in to catch Haskins just about the jawline, spinning him around and against some empty crates. "You need to be educated," snarled Elliott, even as Morrison's hard right fist punched explosively into Haskins's exposed stomach. The reporter cried out in pain and fear and slumped to his knees. The blows kept coming, bruising his ribs and tearing flesh. One came loping in to thud against his left eye, but he barely felt the hard impact as he began sinking into unconsciousness.

Then Joe Elliott grabbed a hunk of hair and

lifted James Haskins's head up where he lay sprawled by the crates. "Hear me good, newspaperman. You've picked the wrong side. This is just a warning. Either change your stories or be prepared for something worse." He let go a sucker punch that struck just about the Adam's apple.

"Come on, Joe, he'll be out a long time."

"Maybe we should finish him off."

"Canton won't like that."

"Yeah," Elliott spat out, "guess he won't." He broke out laughing as he trudged back up the alley and held up his hand to show Ben Morrison the bruised knuckles. "He sure had a hard head."

"Nothing a bullet can't penetrate. I'll buy the first beer."

Around three o'clock a drunk staggering in to take a leak almost tripped over James Haskins's inert body. At first he was under the impression what he had come across was a dead man, this as he took the time to relieve himself. Then he managed to strike flame to a wooden match, and what he found when bending down for a closer look brought him reeling back up the alley and onto Main Street.

In the alley, James Haskins was coming out of it. He'd been aware of the flickering light of the match, and of the man bending over him, and now he summoned enough strength to lift his head up from the hard ground and open his right eye, the left for some reason remaining closed. And now the awful pain came, and he began retching even as he fought to a sitting position. Grabbing for the crates, he pulled to his feet, but spun weakly to bounce against the brick wall.

"Know that man . . . but why . . . why . . ."

Fumbling out his handkerchief, he wiped some of the drying blood away from his mouth, the vague lights from Main Street drawing him that way. "Name . . . can't remember his name . . . oh, it hurts . . ."

Coming onto the boardwalk, he tripped on the planking and fell forward, barely conscious, thinking that just a short distance away was the Occidental Hotel. But in his confusion as he struggled to stay erect, Haskins swung the wrong way, reeling toward the bridge and the swollen waters of the creek.

At this hour most of the saloons had closed, with those still open crowded and boisterous, and it was in one of these that one of Sheriff Red Angus's deputies found himself listening to the drunken ramblings of an out-of-work cowhand. "Tell you, Cliff, found this . . . this gent in that alley . . . all bloody . . . and the hell beat out of him."

Shortly thereafter it was a reluctant deputy sheriff Cliff Pearson leaving a half-finished beer behind who arrived at the bridge and found that the drunken cowhand had been right. He managed to stop James Haskins just short of his tumbling into the creek.

"Damn, mister, you're all beat to hell. Hey, you're that reporter?"

"Hotel . . . Occidental Hotel . . ."

"Haskins, isn't it." He wrapped a brawny arm under James Haskins's shoulders to hold him up, and added worriedly, "You'll be better off in one of my cells. Then I'm fetching a sawbones. Just what happened?" But the next moment the deputy found he was carrying an unconscious man.

"A lot of petty thieves and muggers have drifted

in. But they don't beat a man half to death." thought Cliff.

Once he had placed Haskins on a cot in one of the cells, the deputy threaded through the dark streets of Buffalo and rapped on the front door of a clapboard house. He aroused Doc Andrew Jameson, and within moments the doctor was clothed and going back to the jail. A gruff-spoken man with wide shoulders and big hands suited more for blacksmithing than wielding a scalpel, Jameson told the deputy to go heat up some water as he began removing Haskins's light summer coat. In an inner coat pocket he came across a leathery wallet, and thumbed it open to reveal some folding money.

"Certainly wasn't robbery." Now with some difficulty he managed to pull off the shirt, to survey the bruise marks and place tentative fingers along the ribcage, which brought from James Haskins a shuddering intake of breath.

"Can you hear me, son?" Doc Jameson said. "Take it easy now . . ."

Somehow Haskins blinked his right eye open to focus on the doctor leaning over him, and he said feebly, "Guess I'm in jail."

"A deputy brought you here. Remember that? Anyway, son, you mind telling me what happened?"

"Waylaid . . . by two men."

"I see. From the cut to your clothes you're that reporter who's been moseying around town—Haskins, wasn't it? You're beat up some; but you'll live. Though some ribs might be broken. Any idea who did this to you?"

"I . . . don't know for sure."

But James Haskins knew all too well that one of

his assailants had been a stockmen's association detective. This had been just a brutal warning to clear out of Wyoming. And perhaps he would, but in his own good time. For he wasn't about to slink out of town on any stagecoach. He felt that something other than beating up a reporter was in the wind.

"It's no accident those detectives are up here. They just might have it in mind to gun down some rustlers." His unspoken words were swept aside by the hands of Doc Jameson beginning to administer to his closed left eye, and then let a deep blackness overwhelm him.

Nine

Nine

Ever since they'd come back from Buffalo, it seemed to Nate Champion that everything about this setup just didn't seem to suit Ross Gilbertson. Last night most of Ross's complaining had been that the cabin was too small and if a big winter storm did hit they'd be snowbound out here until spring.

"Man's a habitual bitcher," was Champion's final comment upon finding his bunk.

It took him a while to fall asleep as he kept thinking about the situation he was in. Just a small rancher struggling to get along. Holed up out here in a rented cabin and letting his cattle graze on land not belonging to him. The fact is, mused Nate Champion, all he had were a few horses and a small herd of cattle. He needed a place of his own, but that would mean having to sell off at least half his herd just to buy some land. Life hadn't been all this complicated when he was just a plain cowpuncher. And there was Corrie, giving him the jaundiced eye because her father had him figured to be a rustler. He heard a shuffling sound, opened his eyes to spot the cat gliding across the table and jumping down, then thought to hell with worrying about Ross or anything else and managed to fall asleep.

Sometime before daylight, as was his habit, Nate Champion came awake. He reached down a lazy hand to pet the cat curled up by his bunk, felt the chill of winter penetrating the cabin, and began dozing off again. It could have been fifteen minutes, again a half hour, when the hinged door was flung open and one of those crowding into the cabin said loudly, "We've got you this time, Champion!"

Instantly Champion's eyes popped open and around a shamming yawn he responded with, "What's the matter, boys?" In the palish light darkening the cabin he could make out three vague forms even as he stretched out his left hand for the handgun hanging from the bedpost. The gun slapped into Nate Champion's hand, and he and one of the intruders seemed to fire at the same time, to have a leaden slug powder-burn past Champion's face. Another slug buried into the blankets between the two occupants of the bed.

Nate Champion blazing away again sent the intruders retreating out through the open door. He managed to fire again, whereupon Champion scrambled out of bed and at the door saw one of the assailants clutching at his stomach as he ran into the brush.

Spinning around, Nate Champion yelled at Gilbertson, "Grab your weapon, dammit Ross. There's at least four of those bastards after us." And reluctantly Gilbertson reached for his holstered six-gun and stationed himself by a window.

At the door, Champion stared through the rising light of early morning at a Winchester propped outside against the cabin wall, and a short distance away his own rifle by the woodpile. He knew the attackers would be going for their rifles, and he said to Gilbertson, "I'm going after those rifles—give me some covering fire."

He crouched outside, only to have one of the attackers appear around the corner of the cabin, and Champion managed to jump back inside. Quickly he fired through the chinking of the cabin, and stepping back to the door, he saw the attacker heading into the brush to join the others. "I'm damned if I don't know that coward—that association detective, Joe Elliott. Knew sooner or later they'd try something like this. It was Shonsey telling 'em where to find our cabin. And dammit, Ross, you should have given me some covering fire."

Gilbertson shouted back, "They ain't after me, Nate."

"That's right," retorted Champion, "you're just a damned tumbleweed. When this is over, Ross, I want you packed and out of here. Or better yet, you stay and I'll make other arrangements."

Now it became a waiting game as Nate Champion tried to locate just where those ambushers had gone, as he hadn't heard the sound of their horses. Tiring of this, he scrambled into some clothing and his boots and hat, and leaving a dark look for Gilbertson, he lunged outside to the woodpile. Holstering his sidearm, he made a grab for his Winchester in the chilling light of dawn just marking its presence above the rim of the redstone ledges. Now he broke into the brush, the feeling in Champion that Elliott and his friends had headed out. This proved to be the case when he stumbled upon overcoats and some personal belongings.

"Only one way out of here," he muttered

angrily, "and by now I figure they've used that trail."

He broke back through the brush and hurriedly draped a saddle upon one of the horses. It could be that the attackers would be waiting just outside the narrow fringes of the trail coming into the valley. Mounting up, Nate Champion reined sharply away from the corral, his rifle cradled across his lap and a determined anger in eyes picking out the outward trail.

Later that morning cowpuncher Tommy Carr, working out at what was left of the Bar C, was out in the rundown barn milking a cow when he felt a presence. Turning on the milk stool to glance around the flank of the cow, he discovered it was Nate Champion standing in the open doorway, morning light spilling around Champion and the Winchester he was pointing at Carr.

"Anybody pass this way . . . maybe an hour or so ago?"

"Nope, Nate, ain't seen nobody."

Then Champion was gone, and for a moment Tommy Carr wondered if Champion had even been there at all, and it took some time for Carr's hands to stop shaking before he could settle them upon the bulging tits of the cow.

On the afternoon of the same day Nate Champion, by following shod markings left by the attackers, came upon a hastily abandoned camp on Beaver Creek. Just beyond this, perhaps a mile, lay the NH headquarters, where Mike Shonsey had taken up residence as foreman of the three old British outfits.

Vaulting out of the saddle, Champion took in the gear left behind by the attackers, among the items a bloodstained tarpaulin. "Scored a hit," he

said sourly. "Well, those bastards are long gone."
Ambling over, he sheathed the Winchester and took out the makings and began rolling a cigarette into shape.

"That damned Shonsey set me up. Maybe he was one of the ambushers. But that ain't the sonofabitch's long suit."

Champion rode on, as it had settled in his mind that perhaps he wasn't the only one those attackers were going to call upon. Toward evening he loped in to John A. Tisdale's small spread of buildings. Tisdale's wife looked worriedly out the back door of the log cabin, but recognizing that it was a friend of theirs, she pushed the door open.

"Nate, is something wrong?"

"I guess John isn't here?"

"Went into Buffalo for a few things." She lifted her apron to wipe her hands on it, showing her belly heavy with child under the gingham dress.

His words coming out clipped and angry, Nate Champion related the events of the ambush, adding that he had probably wounded one of the attackers. "It was Joe Elliott for . . ."—he managed to choke off the swear word—"for sure. I figure, Mrs. Tisdale, there's going to be trouble. You know me, I'm good with a gun, but heading up a bunch of men and taking them into a fight is another thing. John, well, he's got the knack."

"You don't think, Nate, they plan to come here?"

"Hard to say, Mrs. Tisdale, as those association boys down in Cheyenne have got their thinkin' all mixed up. I can live with bein' blacklisted. An' even be accused of rustling. But for them to do it this way . . ." He left it there, still fighting mad, frustrated that he hadn't caught up with the ambushers.

"You're more than welcome to stay for supper, Nate." She framed a worried smile, then added, "John should be along anytime."

"Best be heading back."

"Aren't you wintering at the old Hall cabin?"

"Not no more. Just . . . just tell John I'll be by in a couple of days. And to keep a sharp eye out for that damned Joe Elliott . . . and Mike Shonsey, if he's bold enough to come over here. Take care, ma'am."

A week after the attempt on his life, Nate Champion was settled in at the KC ranch. This was actually one of Englishman Moreton Frewen's old line camps. The place had been abandoned yet the huddle of log buildings were still in good shape. It lay along the loop of the Middle Fork, a cutbank stream marked with cottonwoods and box elders and willows.

Yesterday Champion had ridden over to the Hat outfit, and a day later he was heading out for Buffalo. Alongside rode Jack Flagg astride a grulla and expounding on the attempted ambush. "I tell you, Nate, Canton's got to be involved in this."

"We both know he was, Jack."

Jack Flagg's quick laugh was his way of chasing the scowl from Champion's face, and Flagg said, "Must mean they're really running scared. As is Gilbertson."

"Ross sure enough had a shallow bottom," agreed Champion. "Out there his life was on the line too. Wouldn't have been for my cat I'd be pushing up daisies along about now."

"You still think it was Mike Shonsey."

"I know it was."

They set their horses into a ground-eating pace. Jack Flagg pushed down his high-crowned black hat when a cold gust of wind shuddered against him. Both of them wore sheepskins to keep warm. Every so often each man would send out wary glances to distant points. Out here they seemed to be alone, yet the two of them knew careless illusions of this kind often got a man killed.

"You know, Nate, I can't help thinking of what Albert Brock told me . . . back when you looked after his place. He'd left on a trip, came back to find you fixin' to set down at the table in his house . . . and apologizing for the lack of potatoes. So when Brock told you there was a ton of them in his cellar, you replied, yup, I know, Mr. Brock, but they weren't mine."

"I sort of recollect that incident."

"What I'm getting at, Nate, is that you're called rustler simply because you know some. Same's me. I've got to admit from time to time my partners and I acquire some mavericks, as do those uppity-up big ranchers. But calling us rustlers is only more doubledealing by our mutual enemies. You repeat a lie long enough it becomes the truth."

"Meaning we're fair game—same's pronghorns or grizzly bear."

"Open season, Nate."

Nate Champion found upon his arrival at Buffalo that he'd made the front page of Joe DeBarthe's newspaper, and upon emerging from the livery stable, it was DeBarthe calling out to him.

"Nate, got a minute?"

"Barely."

"Ross Gilbertson claims one of the men laying that ambush was Elliott. Care to elaborate on that?"

"It was Elliott." He went on to inform DeBarthe that one of the attackers had been wounded. "Might have brought him in here to get that slug out."

"Worth looking in to, Nate. I see you came in with Flagg. According to the *Cheyenne Leader,* those cattle shipped out by Flagg were impounded."

"Figures," Champion said bitterly. "If so, they impounded the thirty head I sent along."

The editor of the *Buffalo Bulletin* said that although charges of rustling had been brought against six counties, only cattle belonging to Johnson County ranchers had been seized. Further, that the stockmen's commission had issued this order, that if he or Flagg wanted to argue the point, they were privileged to track down to Cheyenne and submit proof of ownership to an ex-parte board.

Joe DeBarthe said, "But that board won't budge an inch to see you getting your money. By the way, Nate, you hear what happened to that Chicago newspaperman?" When Champion allowed that he hadn't, DeBarthe went on, "Guess someone took offense to those stories he's been writing; at any rate, Mr. Haskins got beat up. Claims it was done by some stock detectives."

"I'm sorry this happened," said Champion. "And about them seizing my cattle."

"Just for the record, Nate, Frank Canton headed down to Cheyenne . . . and those stock detectives have left town."

"Won't miss those backjumpers."

Trudging over to Main Street, Nate Champion hesitated in the afternoon sunlight. Way up along the street to the south he picked out the buggy belonging to John A. Tisdale. Between Tisdale and Frank Canton, he knew, were bad feelings that went way back to Texas. John Tisdale hadn't said too much about it, just enough to let Champion and others know that Canton had been involved in some shooting scrapes and had left in one awful hurry, that Canton's real name was Joe Horner. He knew Tisdale to be a proud man, but not a gunfighter as was the ornery and untrustworthy Frank Canton. Whatever the reason, it wouldn't be John Tisdale starting anything, especially since he had four yonkers to raise. And Canton was also a family man, but this hadn't kept the former sheriff of Johnson County from using his gun. If there was a calling out, it was Nate Champion's opinion that Tisdale wouldn't stand a fair chance in a gunfight.

Jack Flagg had said he would meet him at Charlie Chapin's saloon, and Champion started that way. Every so often there'd be a pleasant grin for an acquaintance, and now a frown for Sheriff Red Angus waving from where he lurked inside Stumbo's Restaurant, with Angus striding out to draw Champion aside.

"I expect I know what this is about, Red."

"Ross was in telling most everybody in town what happened. But it was you, Nate, identifying one of those attackers as being Joe Elliott. That being the case, I'm asking you to bring charges against Elliott."

"What good will that do. Elliott gets thrown in the clink; the money boys down in Cheyenne bail him out."

"Now, Nate, don't be so bullheaded," said Angus as he tempered his words with a hasty grin. "It'll show everyone we've got law and order up here. That Johnson County won't stand for any more heavyhanded crap by the cattle kings. Who else was there besides Elliott?"

Recollections came to Champion of how Mike Shonsey had been over near the vicinity of the Hall cabin a couple of days before the attempted ambush. Shonsey knew that country, and though at times he offered the hand of friendship to the smaller ranchers, the man, in the opinion of a lot of people up here, was of Shonsey's being a Judas. "Red, the only man I recognized was Elliott. But there were four of them; one I hit for damned sure."

"That's what Ross Gilbertson told me. Checked with all the local sawbones—haven't treated anyone for a bullet wound of late."

"Figures . . . as there are other towns around. Red, okay, draw up them papers on Elliott. Maybe a few days in your hoosgow will do the sonofabitch some good; though I doubt it."

"You're sure you can't name the others . . ."

"Light wasn't all that certain when they showed up." With a curt nod for the sheriff he went on, the thought in him that sooner or later he'd run into Mike Shonsey.

"Shonsey could have been one of them."

He found the saloon to be packed, and that Jack Flagg hadn't arrived. A lot of gambling was going on, and few people paid any attention to Champion easing to the front end of the bar and dolling out hard coin for a stein of beer. He blew the foam away to drink thirstily. Flicking foam from his drooping mustache, he looked about, and it was

110

then he laid eyes upon Mike Shonsey shuffling a deck of cards at a table beyond the roulette wheels. But Nate Champion held there, sipping at his beer, and noticing that back of Shonsey an empty bench stood along the yellow-plastered wall, while above on the wall was a calendar curling at the edges and three years old. He watched as Shonsey raked in a pot, then began regaling his table companions with some happy words. Champion asked for a refill.

"Winning, Shonsey is still an untrustworthy bastard."

Half-turning, he took a quick glance out onto main street in search of Flagg. He laid eyes upon one of the bardogs, to say quietly, "Ed, keep an eye on my beer."

Champion worked his way among the front tables with the ambling gait of a man looking to sit in on a poker game, and came along the side wall to ease onto the bench behind Mike Shonsey just tossing more chips into the pot. Quietly Nate Champion lifted out his six-gun and leaned forward on the bench, the barrel of his weapon coming to jab ever so gently against the nape of Shonsey's neck, with Shonsey hearing the dry crackling sound of a hammer being thumbed back.

Mike Shonsey stiffened on his chair but otherwise made no attempt to move or drop a hand to his holstered weapon, though he'd paled considerably.

"I want their names, Mike."

"Nate?" he exclaimed just as quietly, "I don't know what this is all about."

Champion had a smile for the other poker players as he said pleasantly, "Go on with your game, gentlemen. Now Mike, Joe Elliott was one of them. Maybe you were one of the others? But in any case you set me up, Shonsey."

"It was Elliott," Shonsey blurted, "and . . . and Canton . . ."

"There were two more."

"Morrison . . . Ben Morrison . . . an' DuFran—"

"I ought to pistol-whip you, Shonsey. Or call you out. But you're just dirty scum." Contemptuously Nate Champion jerked to his feet and shoved the weapon into his holster as he ambled upfront toward the bar and his unfinished stein of beer.

"I . . . I . . ."

The game began breaking up. Sharing how Champion felt toward Shonsey, some of the players simply picked up their chips and left without so much as looking at the cattleman. As for Mike Shonsey, he pocketed his chips and broke for a back door, letting it slam behind him.

Anger still burned Nate Champion's face where he stood at the bar. He'd received little satisfaction in bracing Shonsey, had deliberately done so in here so's to let these people know what manner of men they'd been playing cards with. What Champion resented most of all was that Mike Shonsey didn't have much of a conscience, with Shonsey, as other ranch managers liked to do, sending back book tallies to the absentee owners.

Somehow Nate let his anger die away as, in recalling the earlier conversation with editor Joe DeBarthe, also came thoughts of Corrie . . . and of James Haskins.

Then Jack Flagg stalked into the saloon, drawing Champion aside and coming out with a tirade of angry words about how those cattle he'd shipped out had been impounded by those devils out of Cheyenne. Chipping in with some words of his own, Nate Champion ordered drinks around. A glance out a window would have shown Corrie Middleton saying a few parting words to newspaperman James Haskins.

Only a few purplish vestiges would have told anyone about what had happened to James Haskins's left eye, and but for a small scar near the bridge of his nose, his face was unmarked. He still wore a bandage encircling his ribcage, with any unnecessary activity bringing some pain. The stagecoach had just pulled up, and the shotgun tossed Haskins's luggage up on top.

"I hate leaving, Corrie, but my editors have ordered me to Cheyenne."

"Will I ever see you again, Jim?"

"I care for you more than you realize, Corrie. But until you make up your mind about . . ."

"About Nate? I do care for him . . . and you, James Haskins. Please say you'll come back . . ." She came into his arms.

He drew her close, letting his lips brush her soft hair as James Haskins murmured, "You'll be here?"

"Here and thinking of you."

He clambered aboard as the driver released the brake, and closing the door, James Haskins reached out for her hand. "I'll write, Corrie, I promise."

The horses broke away, leaving puffs of street dust and a young woman looking apprehensively after the stage rolling over a southern rise in the street. She was certain she'd never see James Haskins again.

"He's an Easterner . . . doesn't fit out here, I

113

reckon. But Jim, please come back."

Coming onto sundown they reached the station at Powder River crossing. The passengers got out to partake of an evening meal as the horses were changed. Exiting from the road ranch, James Haskins drew off by himself to gaze upon the Big Horns and about where he figured Buffalo was located.

His friendship with Corrie Middleton had deepened into a relationship which to him meant either asking for her hand in marriage or just leaving. And he had, but only upon orders from Chicago that the big story would be found in Cheyenne. It could be, and this brought some worry, that his unprejudiced stories would be blackballed by the stockmen's association as were a lot of folks up in Johnson County. But he'd found he couldn't slant them otherwise, not after what those stock detectives had done to him. And what about the attack on Nate Champion? What about the association simply taking the money for cattle that had been shipped and so further crippling those just wanting a chance at a better life.

"Cheyenne . . . there's the money and power . . . and just maybe answers to these rumors that an invasion of Johnson County is being considered. Well, so long, Corrie my love. Hope I see you again."

Ten

No longer was it unusual to see H. B. Ijams leaving his suite at the Inter Ocean Hotel sometime after the sun had gone down and returning to his office at the stockmen's association building. Of particular liking to the testy Ijams was that the executive committee had stepped aside to let the power of the association be vested in himself as secretary, and in Major Frank Wolcott and association president John Clay.

"It won't be long," pondered Ijams, "before Clay ventures off to Europe. Which should clear the way to our invading the nest of those damned rustlers. As Clay simply won't agree to it."

He turned onto a side street, and was surprised to see Major Wolcott's buggy lurking out back with some other horses. Then he noticed the lights were on in Wolcott's office. The back door was unlocked, and he entered and removed his hat to pat down his hair before a puzzled frown accompanied him into Wolcott's office and stayed there upon finding those stock detectives had returned from Buffalo.

"Canton," he said briskly, while merely nodding at the others. "I wasn't expecting you back so soon, Frank."

"The Champion situation dictates I be here," said Wolcott, adding that the men in the room had stopped by his ranch on the way up here. "Just what went wrong, Frank?"

"About all that happened is that Nate Champion got lucky," replied Frank Canton. He sat with his legs crossed in one of the chairs, that same haughty expression planted on his angular face. "Word is out, major, that Elliott was recognized; by Champion. I expect charges will be brought."

"Nothing the association can't handle," Ijams said indifferently.

"Yes," Major Wolcott said impatiently, "it'll be taken care of, Joe. But I don't want the same thing happening next time. Which is why Canton will be the only one going back to Buffalo."

"There's a lot of rustlers up there, Major Wolcott," said Ben Morrison. "Meaning we should head up there again."

"I've other plans for you men," said Wolcott. He forced a placating smile. "The secretary and I have plans. Mr. Canton, when you get back, I do believe it advisable you throw a little scare into these rustlers. Perhaps gunning down one or two will do the job."

"I know some I'd like to take out," said Frank Canton. "But just what kind of backing do I have in this? The law up there isn't on our side."

"Gentlemen, I'll tell you now that every member has donated a thousand dollars toward getting rid of these rustlers—one hundred thousand dollars to be precise. To be used for the express purpose of gathering an army."

"About time," grinned Phil DuFran.

"This will take time," Wolcott said. "Meanwhile you men and our other detectives out in the field will continue gathering evidence against these rustlers. There is one other matter." Picking up an envelope, he thrust it at Joe Elliott. "You and DuFran will be heading over to Newcastle. There you'll get together with Fred Coates."

"Nothing much happens in Newcastle," protested Elliott.

"That is about to change." A curt nod from Major Wolcott sent the pair of stock detectives retreating from his office, and then Wolcott brought his swivel chair around to face Frank Canton. After relating to Canton the task he had in mind, Canton nodded through cold eyes.

"I'll make sure the men you wanted killed are on our blacklist. Perhaps this just might discourage these rustlers until we get some men together and head up there."

"Your ranch is up there, Frank. Pulling our other men out might give these rustlers false assurances that we've given up. But to the contrary, men."

H. B. Ijams said, "The major and I have sent inquiries down to Texas. What we need are former lawmen willing to join our army." Ijams related as to how stock detective Tom Smith had been sent down there to recruit gunfighters, and that tomorrow he and Morrison would depart for Idaho with the same purpose in mind.

When Frank Canton finally left the association building, it was to find a hotel, and afterward a quiet saloon. He'd been allowed to look at the blacklist, but Canton didn't need this list as he'd

117

already decided who he would kill first.

"John Tisdale has got to go. As he knows things about me that I want buried. Yup, it's Tisdale."

Cheyenne was as James Haskins had last seen it, a large town sustained by the Union Pacific Railroad and home to many of the cattle kings. The ride up through Powder River country had been uneventful, with a brief stop at Casper before he'd boarded a train to arrive here yesterday afternoon. Instead of checking in at the Commodore, he had found a modest hotel a short distance away from the stockyards. Then a buggy ride to the post office for his mail, which turned out to be another letter of instructions from his editors. Armed with this, Haskins had gone to a nearby saloon to partake of a supper of cold cuts and cheese chased down with beer.

Instead of drab Eastern garb, James Haskins's lanky frame was encased in a cattleman's leather coat and flannel shirt, the snug trousers fitting over spurless boots and the hat formed to his liking, the brim sweeping up at the sides and low in front to shield the reflective glimmer in his eyes. He'd picked up a few Western mannerisms, felt more at ease in what he was wearing. Had acquired a new slant of augering out things, such as why those stock detectives had left Buffalo to wind up here.

"Maybe to let things cool down after they tried to take out Nate Champion."

But reporter James Haskins felt it was more than this, which was the reason he left to find the Golden Steer Bar, just a block away from the Cheyenne Club and where most of the newspapermen hung out. He recognized some of the local reporters, skimming over a lot of men in Eastern suits and derbies or felt hats before he made his way back to the pool tables.

"Howdy, Shaunsey. Seems you still have trouble banking those balls."

"Howdy . . . Haskins, is that you?"

"In the flesh."

"Man, I thought you went back to Chicago."

"Been doing some traveling."

"Appears so," grinned Art Shaunsey as he dropped his cue on the table and thrust out a hand. "I like your getup."

"Come on, I need to pick your brain."

Art Shaunsey, a reporter for the *Boston Herald,* ambled after Haskins to the bar, where they wedged into a place and were soon throwing questions at one another around steins of beer. "Hold on, Jim, you were up at Buffalo?"

"Fascinating place."

"The stronghold of the rustler, I hear."

"Mostly the home of a lot of honest men. Art, something's in the wind."

"The stockyards are thataway." Shaunsey laughed and gulped down some beer. The smile fading away, he realized the man he had shared a lot of drinks with had changed, noticed for the first time the slight puffiness around the left eye and the scar, that somehow James Haskins looked a little older. "Okay, Jim, fire away."

"First I'll tell you what I know, Art. Seems a bit out of sorts all those stock detectives coming in here."

"Come to think on it, Jim, a lot of hard-eyed men have been drifting in and out of the stockmen's association building the last couple of days. You were up at Buffalo? Then you'll know about this attempted killing . . . this Champion?"

"I figure the same men making an attempt to kill Nate Champion beat the hell out of me."

"The hell you say, Jim?"

"Didn't like my editorials, I reckon."

"Got to admit, Mr. Haskins, your editorials have riled up a lot of people down here. Some are swearing to bring libel charges against you."

James Haskins laughed and said, "When all I'm telling is the truth. What they want is to whitewash my newspaper. Got word that some of these cattle kings have written to my editors about this."

"Consider this, my friend, they might administer something worse than a beating next time."

"That could be. Well, you've been keeping tabs on the stockmen's association down here."

"Jim, I go over there, either Ijams or Major Wolcott issues a statement, then we see it's printed. But these stock detectives love their hard liquor. When in their cups a lot of dirt comes out. They're an underhanded bunch, doing the bidding of Wolcott, which isn't keeping this country safe for democracy but protecting the interests of the cattle kings. By any means, Jim, foul or dishonest."

"What worries me is this Cattle Kate thing, Art. The ranchers who did it going scot-free because all of the witnesses are either dead or missing. It boils down to one thing—here in Wyoming the law is being manipulated by the cattle kings. Which will only lead to more killing."

"Aren't you stretching this a mite?"

"I wish I were, Art. I truly do. But it isn't just this Maverick Law anymore . . . or a few cattle being rustled. Now it comes down plain and simple to the cattle kings wanting complete control of all that happens out here. Get rid of the homesteader, small rancher, or anybody else standing in their way. There'll be more killings. And they'll get up an army and invade Johnson County. Can't afford not to, the way I figure it."

"A helluva mouthful, Mr. Haskins," whistled the other newspaperman. "Just hope what you said doesn't get back to Major Wolcott or his cronies. But after due consideration, you're right."

"And what will you place on paper, Mr. Shaunsey?"

"As you are so fond of saying, Jim, where's the truth of the matter?"

"Stick close, Mr. Shaunsey, if you dare," came James Haskins's reckless words. "There are some men recently come to Cheyenne I intend to interview. Elliott or Morrison or Canton—whoever I run into first."

"These names make me a trifle uneasy."

"Yup, Shaunsey, they're packing guns and know how to use them. But our weapon is the power of the press. You coming?"

"It seems to me that hot lead cuts through paper," said the other reporter. "But what the hell, a little excitement is just what I need."

Shortly before reporters Haskins and Art Shaunsey had arrived to station themselves in the shadows across from the stockmen's association building, a trio of stock detectives had left to head downtown. But their vigilance was rewarded with the appearance of Frank Canton. They let Canton amble upstreet about a half-block before taking out after him, with Canton quartering to the southeast on the dark streets of Cheyenne and then pulling up under a street lamp.

Frank Canton had on a Gus-style hat and yellow slicker hanging just above the silvery-gleaming spurs on his high-heeled boots. The slicker was open to show, as he turned for a cautious backward glance, the holstered Colt's .45 and fancy shirt under the cattleman's coat. There was a vague blustering of wind along the streets, nipping coldly at exposed flesh.

"What's he holding up for?"

Haskins whispered back, "That's Canton's way."

"I've heard a few things about Canton."

"They're probably all true, as he can use that gun."

"Jim, you sure you want to go through with this?"

"Yup," he said quickly.

"Man, I had plans to head back to Boston this weekend. But as an Irishman to one stubborn Scotsman, what have I got to lose, outside of my tenuous hold on this life, that is."

"Don't be so damned melodramatic," smiled Haskins. "There, he's crossing over to that saloon. You go in first and find a convenient place to view the illustrious Frank Canton. Then I'll be there to converse with the former sheriff of Johnson County."

"What if he isn't in a talking mood, James?"

"Get the lead out."

Heading out, Shaunsey threw back, "May the saints be with me."

When both men had entered the saloon, the Central Bar & Billiard Parlour, James Haskins passed the intersection and the revealing street light to draw up just outside one of the wide front windows adorned with gothic printing and pierced by a couple of bullet holes that had been plugged with bits of reddish cloth. He couldn't help thinking of his days at Buffalo, that the man inside, Canton, could have been one of those hammering away at him with his naked fists. For certain one of them had been Joe Elliott, and the sudden anger that surfaced brought a mustering of resolve when he shouldered through the door.

For a Thursday night the saloon was crowded, but he had little difficulty in picking out Frank Canton and that yellow slicker of his back by those playing faro. Canton had pushed the brim of his hat back and was sucking cigarette smoke into his mouth. His narrowed eyes still wore that watchful glint. James looked about in the deeper shadows near the back of the large room and among the tables for Art Shaunsey, thinking for a moment Shaunsey could have slipped out the back door.

"Not that Irishman," he murmured as he strolled toward the man he was seeking on a floor covered with sawdust and debris. "Canton, you got a minute?"

Frank Canton spun around lightly on his boots to lay unreadable eyes upon a man he'd last seen in Buffalo. "Not for you," he finally said.

"Not so fast, Canton," he said just as rudely. "Elliott and someone else, maybe you, ganged up on me back there. Gave me these. All because someone didn't like what I've been saying in my newspaper, the *Chicago Gazette*."

Canton laughed mirthlessly, then cut it off to say, "Elliott is his own man. You're Haskins?"

"You damnwell know my name, Canton," he said.

"Why don't we go out back and discuss this?"

"That back table is my choice," countered Haskins, and he went ahead of the gunfighter, fighting down his sense of unease as he did so. Warily he pulled out a chair and eased onto it as Canton sat down, suggestively pulling the slicker out of the way of his holstered six-gun.

"No, Haskins, I don't like what you've been saying in that rotten paper of yours. Neither do a lot of my friends."

"Then you don't like the truth."

A hard smile served to lift Canton's mustache and show the yellowed teeth. "It seems you are a fool after all. And much more than that, Haskins, you're dangerous."

"I'm not packing a gun, Canton. Before leaving Buffalo, I had a talk with Nate Champion. He said you were one of those who paid him a visit."

Recklessly, the anger in him spilling out, James Haskins went on, "And here in Cheyenne, Canton, your bosses told you about their plans to invade Johnson County . . . or you'll deny this, as you've denied a lot of other things."

The Colt's appeared without warning, though it was shielded from those closer to the front of the saloon. Frank Canton murmured quietly:

"Perhaps something of this nature is being planned. If so, let it happen. But you, as I've said before, are a dangerous man. Just want you to know I saved your life before . . . countermanded those orders to have you taken care of—a mistake, I've come to realize. Now, just take it slow and easy, Haskins, and we'll go out that back hallway."

"Not so fast, Canton."

The gunfighter, who'd just started to shove up

from his chair, held there as the barrel of Art Shaunsey's .32 pistol nudged into his back. Carefully he lowered his Colt to place it on the table. Now he swiveled his eyes back to Haskins. "Perhaps we'll meet again?"

"Perhaps we will," he replied. "I expect you'll be heading back to Buffalo?"

There was a hesitant nod from Canton. "Soon, I expect."

"Give my regards to Nate Champion." Slipping around the table, Haskins headed for the front door with Art Shaunsey a step behind and the six-gun shoved into a coat pocket. They wasted little time in hurrying away from the saloon and back to Haskins's hotel and the barroom.

"Did you see his eyes?"

He slumped down next to Shaunsey on a bar stool. "I don't want to see them again." This time James Haskins ordered a bottle of whiskey, requesting that it be left before them on the bar. "He more or less confirmed the rumors about this invasion. And that the orders he received . . ."

"Those to get rid of you, Jim?"

"Yup, that they came from Cheyenne, from here, dammit." Now he found that he was trembling, and it was with some difficulty he managed to pour whiskey into their shot glasses.

"Whatever," muttered Shaunsey as he downed the contents of his shot glass, then quickly refilled it. "I'm expected back in Boston. And if you had any sense, Jim my man, you'd be on the same train."

"Can't, Art, can't leave now. Too much has happened, to me and a lot of other folks out here. Guess matters are coming to a boiling point, this situation between the cattle kings and the men they call rustlers. Just have to stick it out."

"Then let us get pleasantly drunk together, Jim my man, as we did come out alive from that encounter with Canton, which means my prayers to the saints were answered. Here, Jim, don't be sitting there with an empty glass."

"Thanks, Art, for saving my bacon back there."

Shaunsey lifted out his small handgun in the dimness of the small barroom, spun the cylinder, and suddenly went ashen as he exclaimed, "Oh man, I cleaned it this morning, but forgot to reload the damned thing."

Nervous laughter broke out between them. "You'd better head back for Boston."

"But I'm leaving this with you, James Haskins, as I've a feeling you'll need it. Now let's do some serious drinking and soul-searching."

Eleven

East of Newcastle in Weston County in fledging Wyoming lay the dark-stippled Black Hills. Stretching west of this cow town were the Great Plains, with a few heights such as Pumpkin Buttes and farther northwest a huge volcanic rock known as Devil's Tower. In between these humps of land one could find verdant grazing land. Cattle far outnumbered horses except in a large pasture owned by settler Thomas Waggoner.

The Waggoner place wasn't all that far from Newcastle, where it was more'n rumored that Waggoner was a receiver of stolen horses. But Waggoner didn't have time to worry about such things as public opinion as he had upwards of a thousand horses to take care of, and a wife and two children, a boy of around four, and the baby.

His small squalor of buildings had been termed a pig sty by unfriendly neighbors, who'd also let out that Thomas Waggoner's wife was brain damaged. But little did the settler care as long as the woman kept the kids out from underboot, and tended to the washing and cooking.

Waggoner had a way of always looking over his

shoulder as if his past was catching up with him, and he was scrawny and long-limbed, wore greasy clothing, this being a faded woolen shirt worn at the elbows and bib overalls so's he could jab his thumbs into their upper ends and be reassured his big, fat wallet was there. Strapped around his thin waist was a gunbelt holding up a Peacemaker, the fretting worry in him today that those horse buyers would camp over someplace instead of heading in. For Waggoner wanted to unload some horses, as his pasture was overcrowded.

"Should'a been here by now."

He looked about his place with the eyes of a man who knew chores had to be done but was just too damned lazy to care. In a shed he had started up a still, turning out some prime lightning, as he called it. He went there now to check on things, and picking up a jug of whiskey and hefting his Winchester, he ambled outside to move slowly to a nearby hump of land shaded by an oak tree. Halfway there it came to Waggoner that he'd left his big, fat wallet back in the cramped bedroom he shared with his wife and young'uns, but he gave a lazy shrug and trudged on.

Now another interruption came as three horsemen suddenly wheeled out of a gap in some distant hills and loped toward Thomas Waggoner, pulling up as he debated if these were the horse buyers.

"Long's they've got hard cash," he muttered, as with a weary sigh he turned around and headed in.

Closer to the buildings he realized the arrivals were men he hadn't seen before, and he took a firmer grip on his rifle. He didn't like the way they had fanned out but still came in steadily, now

128

walking their horses. It was Joe Elliott calling out first and waving.

"Howdy—you Mr. Waggoner?"

"I could be," he said guardedly. Dressed too fancy to be hoss traders, was Waggoner's silent comment, the next moment to find himself facing three drawn handguns. "Now just what in tarnation is going on?"

"This here"—Joe Elliott exposed the warrant given to him by Major Wolcott—"is a warrant for your arrest. The charge is stealing horses."

"I got them hosses honestlike. Got bills of sale for them."

"Waggoner, you'll have to tell that to the judge next session of court. You planning on using that rifle?"

The settler hesitated, as he was angry at himself for letting this happen. Other times at the approach of anyone he would be holed up in one of the buildings, and he exclaimed bitterly, "Guess you ain't hoss traders." He threw the rifle down but still kept his hold on the whiskey jug. "What's it to be now, jail over at that damned Newcastle . . ."

Phil DuFran swung his handgun that way when Waggoner's wife let the storm door slam behind her. Her husband called out angrily, "Get my damned wallet, woman, as these are damned lawmen. Need bail money, I reckon."

"No," stated DuFran as he wheeled his horse over and waved at the woman to go back into the house. "Your husband won't be needing any wallet."

They made Thomas Waggoner pick out and saddle his own horse, as the settler still didn't harbor any suspicions these were anything but bona fide starpackers. Setting off away from the buildings, at first it was in the general direction of Newcastle. DuFran, keeping to the rear, had untied the riata from a saddle thong, and was even smiling as he began fastening a hanging knot. The other detectives rode on either side of the settler, staying close to him. They hadn't bound Waggoner's arms, but his holster was empty, and now Elliott twisted to look back at DuFran. He could see Elliott's eyes nudging toward a cottonwood a short distance ahead.

Joe Elliott took out a pair of handcuffs and said pleasantly to the settler, "Sometimes we've got certain regulations to follow." He made Waggoner rein up, and then Elliott brought the man's arms behind his back to snap on the handcuffs. Giving Waggoner a friendly pat on the back, the three men up front headed out again.

To Waggoner's right, on a bronc having an OX brand, rode stock detective Fred Coates, who'd kept quiet until now. Clearing his throat, Coates said, "Waggoner, all you are is a mangy horse thief."

The settler's reaction was to swear and flare back at Coates, "Just who are you to pass judgment? Thought that was up to the judge. You damned lawmen with your tinny little badges are all one and the same. Say, just where are those badges?"

The answer Thomas Waggoner received was the rope just cast by Phil DuFran spilling down over his neck as Elliott yanked the reins from Waggoner. Elliott matched every cuss word just uttered by the settler.

". . . thief and worse, that's what you are, Waggoner. We're duly appointed stock detectives. As such, you damned thief, we're authorized to pass judgment as we see fit."

Quickly Phil DuFran tossed the other end of the lasso over a high branch, then he sidestepped his horse over and wrapped it around the trunk of the cottonwood to pull the slack out.

Coates asked, "Any last words?"

"Just hang the sonofabitch!" chortled DuFran.

And Joe Elliott complied with a pleased smile as he whipped the horse out from under Thomas Waggoner to leave the settler dangling and spinning around under the high branch of the cottonwood. They watched until, with a last expelling of air, Waggoner went limp.

"Damn, Joe, we should have let Waggoner bring along his wallet."

"Should have. Well, boys, that was a fine piece of work. Hanging a man always did make me thirsty. I'll buy when we get to Newcastle."

And they headed out to leave settler Thomas Waggoner hanging from a tree scarcely two miles from his house.

Among other things the news of the hanging also brought the comment from the Weston County sheriff that he had been planning to go out and arrest Thomas Waggoner for possessing stolen horses. Since Newcastle was far removed from Powder River country, the death of Waggoner was soon forgotten.

Up in Johnson County and in neighboring counties, burned-over brands were beginning to appear, as were dead cows. And there were men going about killing other men's cattle and selling the meat to the army posts and the Burlington grading crews. The fall roundups saw rustlers working in twos or threes, as they worked ahead of the roundup to hide small bunches of cattle, let the cattle drive pass them by, and then head back to brand these stolen cattle. These criminals stole from both the cattle kings and the small outfits.

Down in Cheyenne, James Haskins's *Chicago Gazette* and other newspapers had become aware of the situation up north, though Major Wolcott and the stockmen's association kept branding everyone a rustler.

And as early December arrived, Jim Haskins turned restive eyes northward past the Laramies to be overcome with thoughts of Buffalo and Corrie Middleton.

"To spend Christmas with her," he murmured pensively.

But it was in the saloons of Cheyenne and a few furtive visits to the Cheyenne Club that he'd picked up talk by the cattle kings of their intentions to finally bring an end to the rustling. Sometimes Jim would see these men going into the gun shops to purchase fancy rifles, his inquiries revealing the association was footing the bill for these weapons. Secretary Ijams, he'd also learned, and stock detective Ben Morrison, were out in Idaho. There was also the puzzling fact of association president Clay departing for Europe.

"This would more or less leave Major Wolcott in charge," pondered Jim Haskins. "A man whose vulturine statements in the newspapers left little doubt as to the bitter feelings he had for the rustlers. When, when will it happen, this invasion?" Haskins knew all he could do was to keep digging out anything that might tip the hand of Major Wolcott. Another source of information had been a telegraph operator telling Jim Haskins of wires being exchanged between Texas and the association office in Cheyenne.

And Jim Haskins had heeded reporter Shaunsey's advice and taken to packing around that .32 revolver. Though Frank Canton had left some time ago to return to Buffalo, the man had friends here.

"Yup, this place is no different than Buffalo . . . where a man has to pick sides. Right about now I don't know if I picked the right one or not. As there's a lot of honest men on either side of the fence."

Twelve

The arrival of December to Buffalo meant that court was in session and ranchers were there to lay in supplies for the winter. Just a sprinkling of snow dusted the approaches to town and held in spots on rooftops. A few leaves still clung to the skeletal branches of cottonwoods and oaks and lesser trees sprinkled around the buildings, with the unchanging firs a carpet of green on the lower slopes of the Big Horns, and above that the jagged peaks.

The weather had held for most of last month, and was expected to stay about the same up until the Christmas holidays, though there were always a few ranchers grousing that a good snowfall would help to wet up the parched land hereabouts.

Even though it seemed to the casual observer there was a general feeling of goodwill filtering through the streets, nobody went out of his way to be overly friendly, or to call anyone a shaded name even in jest. Everyone expected Nate Champion or that Flagg outfit to show up, as did Sheriff Red Angus, for he'd served those papers on Joe Elliott, only to have the man post bail and skedaddle out of Johnson County.

Of the smaller ranchers, young settler and bronc buster Orley Jones had come in. Known to everyone as Ranger, he had arrived in his buckboard, as Ranger Jones was going to purchase floorboards for a new house he was building out at his homestead on the Red Fork. Just below his place lay the Hat outfit. Another Texan, he fitted right in with Jack Flagg and his partners.

"When's the wedding, Ranger?"

"Soon's them floorboards are laid, it'll take place. I do want to thank you boys for asking me along last night." He'd gone over to a dance at Piney, a settlement just north of Buffalo, and though he refrained from drinking, Ranger knew word would probably get back to his intended.

The five of them were settled around a table in the Cowboy Saloon. For Ranger Jones it was a cup of chicory coffee, the other cowhands sipping away at steins or shot glasses and partaking in idle talk. Earlier Chuck Meador had mentioned his seeing two of their avowed enemies, Frank Canton and rancher Fred Hesse, perched in Hesse's buggy as he wheeled it in toward the Occidental Hotel. Right away Meador had been sorry that he'd brought up Hesse's name, as all of them knew that Ranger Jones had had words with Hesse to the effect that if that sonofabitch Hesse goes for his gun, I'll plug him full of holes. This happened some time ago at a local saloon, with Hesse simply walking away. And it wasn't any drunken brag as Ranger Jones didn't drink or smoke.

"Look," Ranger Jones began in the manner of a man wanting to get something off his chest, "it isn't so much Hesse as what he stands for. I homesteaded according to the laws of this state . . . and federal laws. Even so, if I so much as look sideways at a cow or maverick, it means to Hesse I'm a rustler. It rankles the hell out of me, boys, and—and, it just ain't right."

"It's hard to swallow, that's for damned sure, Ranger. Me, got laid off last month, as Harv and Mel did. There's work in Butte, the copper mines. But a slow death."

"Hesse, him and Canton are closer than peas in a pod."

"Canton had to be one of those trying to take out Nate."

"Had to be, but Champion's been awful tight-lipped about it."

"The way Nate can handle that gun of his, wouldn't surprise me none him taking the law into his own hands."

"Canton's fast."

"No match for Nate Champion."

Ranger Jones set his cup aside and rose to cast a speculative glance outside. His sighting in on the Occidental Hotel revealed that either Fred Hesse was gone or he'd stabled his horse pulling that buggy. Then Ranger glanced upward to take in the sky paled by a few clouds. Stating his intentions to head back to his place, he shook hands all around and left.

In about a half-hour Ranger Jones left town driving his two-horse buckboard laden down with floorboards and other provisions. The road he ventured south on hugged the low first ridge of the mountains called the Horn. Later on it would swing westward far to the south and inch along a low pass and the settlements of Barnum and Riverside. Beyond that lay the Red Fork and his homestead.

"Fred Hesse, man shouldn't get under my skin so much. But I just can't help it . . . as no man wants to be called a thief."

It was closing on sundown when he encountered a sheepman named Kingsbury just north of the crossing of Muddy Creek, this about fifteen miles south of Buffalo. He waved and the sheepman called out:

"Gonna be awful dark by the time you get home, Ranger."

"Should have started out earlier. You heading for town?"

"That I am. You take care now, Ranger."

Passing on the opposite way, it wasn't long before the sheepman detected movement a short distance away to the north. He could make out what he thought to be a freighter looking for his work animals, though the man was astride a fine horse and carried a rifle.

"None of my concern," the sheepman finally muttered as he jabbed his spurs to bring his bronc into a lope to carry him over a hillock.

About a mile before coming onto the bridge, Ranger Jones, burdened down with his heavy load and with night pressing in, returned the nervous wave of a homesteader's wife sawing at the reins of a horse pulling a wagon. Huddled next to her on the seat was her son, and though seeing someone else out here had been comforting, she knew that Buffalo was still a considerable distance away. Most of the worry was for the two hundred dollars in her purse, money that she'd use to buy supplies for the winter.

The boy stirred on the seat, and she blurted out nervously, "Don't start fretting now, Chad. It's hard enough keeping to the road."

Coming over a rise, a frightened hand went to her throat as there appeared before her a horseman, with the bandanna tied over his face, sending fear tremors passing through her as of a coyote running over one's grave. Somehow she managed to drop her purse and kick it under the loose hay strewn on the bottom of her wagon. A protective arm going around her son's quavering shoulders, she pulled him close as the rider went past at a slow canter.

Casting a backward glance over her shoulder, there flared in her eyes a spark of recognition for the way the horseman sat in his saddle, ramrod straight, not with the casual slouch of a cattleman. The horse seemed to flame some remembrance too, but fearful of any man wearing something to shield who he was, she whipped her horse into a lope that carried it away.

Frank Canton didn't bother to steal a look back at the woman in the wagon as he brought his horse off the road to cut around to the north and kept from being spotted by Ranger Jones still about a quarter of a mile from the bridge over Muddy Creek and bringing his horses along at a laboring walk. Canton wasn't alone, as he'd sent Fred Hesse on ahead to act as a decoy. Another reason was that one of the horses harnessed to Jones's wagon was green broke, and once he opened up with his rifle, it could try to break away.

Now that he was ahead of the wagon on the road, Frank Canton cut back through a gully and reached the bridge, to bring his horse under it. Beyond the bridge about twenty feet he could make out in the deepening darkness of night how the road passed through a cut, and he muttered upon unsheathing his rifle:

"That's where Hesse should be waiting."

Canton took a firmer grip on the reins when the rumble of Ranger Jones's heavy wagon vibrated on the bridge planking as he went over it. Levering a shell into the breech of his rifle, Canton brought it to his shoulder and sighted in on the man perched on the wagon seat, but refrained from pulling the trigger.

Ranger Jones, huddled in his sheepskin and lost in a reverie of thoughts, suddenly became aware of a rider appearing seemingly out of nowhere, and through blinking eyes he called out as he sawed on the reins to halt his wagon and pair of horses:

"You plumb woke me up, mister." It wasn't until the horseman had moved in closer to within about an arm's length of his horses that he knew who it was, and Ranger Jones blurted out, "Hesse, what the hell is this?"

The answer Ranger Jones received was the impact of a rifle bullet striking his cartridge belt. Then he realized it wasn't Hesse but someone behind him. But it didn't matter, nor was there time to unlimber his own weapon, as another .44-40 caliber slug punched into his side, and another into his chest, for somehow Ranger Jones had twisted around on the seat, with both slugs mortal wounds. The next moment his body had sprawled down on the wide seat.

The ambushers brought Ranger Jones's rig off the road some three hundred yards, unhitched the horses, and turned them loose.

"What do you think?"

"The job is done," Canton said matter-of-factly. "Don't be getting second thoughts as Jones was a known rustler."

"Who else you got in mind to kill, Frank?"

"Best you don't know."

"Though it was you pulling the trigger"—Fred Hesse took a lingering glance at the body left behind on the wagon seat—"it still shakes a man up. But as you said, out here rustling is a killing offense."

Thirteen

The passage of another day found Texan John
A. Tisdale making that long trek to Buffalo. A
man with a sober bent of mind, he set about
gathering supplies that he hoped would carry him
through until spring. But even as John Tisdale
tended to this, in him were bitter reminiscences of
all that trouble Frank Canton had caused for him
back in Texas. He liked it here, as it had the comforting presence of the Big Horns and other
Texans. But every time he had occasion to come
into Buffalo, it was with the bitter expectancy of
running into Canton. Somehow the men had
avoided one another and further trouble.

Presently Tisdale's wagon and team of horses
were left at one of the livery stables, but he'd
brought along a list of what he needed. The bulk of
his supplies he'd bought from Bobby Foote, a man
who'd become a close friend and sometime confi-
dant, though John Tisdale never mentioned to
Foote that he even knew Canton. Turning downstreet, he muttered ponderingly:

"Yes, before I forget, the hardware store has
gotten in some new shoes and special nails; might

try them out." He tipped his hat to some passing women as he stepped onto the boardwalk and crossed it to enter Carlton's Hardware Store, a place where he'd opened a charge account.

But the greeting John Tisdale received from the owner of the store brought a frown rippling across his face. "Something wrong, Mr. Carlton?" Tisdale asked.

"The truth is, Tisdale, I can't let you charge anymore . . . from now on, it's cash on the barrelhead."

"Hell, Carlton, I've got a savings account over to the bank," he said curtly.

"It isn't that you can't pay, Tisdale, it's . . . it's . . ."

"Spell it out for me."

"It boils down to this: I deal with the homesteaders and such and . . . and I don't get the trade of the big ranchers. I need their business, Tisdale—you understand."

"When did this all come about?" he asked bitterly.

"Bunch of them came in . . . last week, yeah, a week ago. I tried arguing with them, but you know Canton . . ."

Just the mention of Frank Canton's name caused Tisdale to turn away from the counter and he threw back, "I'll be back directly to pay off my bill—soon's I draw some money out of the bank."

John Tisdale tried shoving aside the terrible anger, even as he went over and bought some Christmas presents for his children. This time he paid for his purchases in money just drawn out of the bank, then left what he'd bought there as he headed outside and back toward the livery stable.

"Canton . . . that damned Canton . . . some-

144

thing'll happen if I hang around here . . . in a place I'm not wanted." Part of him tried bringing out the fact that he wasn't the only small rancher being blackballed by those big ranchers, but John Tisdale's anger just kept on simmering, and others couldn't help noticing this as Tisdale trudged past them on the crowded street.

Suddenly he pulled up short, as just coming off a side street and turning into the Old Court Saloon was the focus of his blinding anger. He broke into a long striding walk, unaware that only yesterday Frank Canton had killed a man in cold blood, and unmindful of the fact he wasn't carrying a weapon, just big hands clenching into fists. He entered the saloon, with the door he'd flung open slamming against the inside wall and rattling windowpanes. The noise brought the eyes of those at the tables his way. And then he was at the bar and spinning a startled Frank Canton around.

Tisdale was a lot bigger than the former sheriff, and he used his size now to backhand Canton away from the bar as he blurted out, "I tried forgetting a lot of things, Canton. As to what happened down in Texas. That you're no big gunhand"—a slapping hand knocked Canton's hat away—"but a dirty little back-shooter."

Frank Canton had little choice but to stumble backward as he tried to evade Tisdale's flailing hands. He could have reached for his holstered gun, but everyone here knew that John Tisdale never carried one. Abruptly Canton broke away from a table and ran for the back door. Tisdale made no effort to follow Canton outside, since for the first time he became aware of what he had just done, and of everyone there stonewalling their eyes at him. Now he felt out of place, and his face reddened, but instead of explaining his actions, John Tisdale simply left.

He found another saloon at the opposite end of the street and a bottle of whiskey. Under the influence of whiskey, the anger in John Tisdale began to take the shape of worry. And the whiskey began to loosen his tongue, to have Tisdale talk freely now of what he'd done, and of how he felt that an attempt would be made on his life.

To an acquaintance he said, "I know Canton better'n most. He won't let this slip. I got a six-gun, but it's stowed in my wagon."

"Now John, forget this talk of guns . . . and Frank Canton. You're not a drinker, you know . . . and me and Mildred have got a spare bedroom, which you're welcome to bunk in."

Blinded to everything but his hatred for Frank Canton, he blundered outside to find another saloon.

It was here in the Senate Saloon that he ran into Tommy Carr, who'd just quit out at the Bar C, while coming in a little later was a cowboy in charge out at the Cross H, Elmer Freeman. Both of these men headed over to Tisdale's table. By evening John Tisdale should have quit drinking and gone someplace to sleep it off, but he held in there, buying both of the cowhands drinks and expressing his fears that he would be ambushed on the way out to his place.

To this Tommy Carr said, "You want, John, I'll head out with you in the morning."

Drunkenly he replied, "I'm not ready to leave yet." Eyeing Carr's six-gun, he added, "Need a gun . . . a big one . . ." Shoving up from the table, and muttering that he would be back, Tisdale left the saloon.

Across the way stood Gus Carlton's big hardware store, but he bypassed the wooden frame building and in the next block went into a hardware business run by a man named George Munkres. The hardware dealer was alone, and in a sort of drunken tirade John Tisdale told of his encounter with Canton, and of his fears, and that he wanted to purchase a shotgun. In his drunken stupor Tisdale had forgotten that Munkres was a close friend of Frank Canton's, as Munkres said with a false show of concern:

"I'd certainly be alarmed too, Mr. Tisdale. A shotgun, you say?"

"And shells for it."

"Say, Mr. Tisdale, those yonkers of yours wouldn't be wanting a puppy and its ma . . ." Munkres went behind a counter and lifted from the floor a small black and white dog. "Just a couple of months old; cute little thing."

"Wolves did scare off my dog," Tisdale admitted.

"I tell you what, Mr. Tisdale, you take the dogs, I'll knock five dollars off the cost of the shotgun—and throw in a free box of shells."

"Okay, but you hold on to them dogs until I'm ready to leave. But I'll take the shotgun now."

From a gun rack the hardware dealer lifted out a shotgun and placed it on the counter where Tisdale was standing. With a placating smile he said, "Store the shells in a back room."

"Better make that two boxes."

Munkres stepped around to a back door, where he brought light to a lamp as it was nearing sundown. He could scarcely believe his luck in John Tisdale coming in here. Nor could he believe the man had taken to drink, but as Canton was a close

147

personal friend, what came to the mind of George Munkres at that moment was his notion of helping out Canton. He found what he wanted in the form of a shell crimper and used the hand-held tool on a box of shotgun shells, tampering with the metal ends so that the firing pin of the shotgun wouldn't strike it solidly. This would probably cause a misfire if the shell fired at all. Quickly he tampered with all the shells in both boxes. Sealing the boxes up again, he brought them out and set them down by the shotgun. It had occurred to Munkres in a vague sort of way that what he had just done was probably consigning a man to death. But, as he'd chosen to be on the side of Canton and the cattle kings, he brushed aside any stirrings of conscience.

"There you be, Mr. Tisdale. Yes, that'll do." He handed the rancher a few greenbacks in change. "Don't forget those dogs now . . . and enjoy the rest of your stay here."

To be publicly humiliated was something that Frank Canton never expected would happen to him, and the seeds of revenge were riding with Canton on the way out of Buffalo. Even George Munkres telling him about selling Tisdale those tampered shotgun shells brought no smile tugging at Canton's mouth. He was out to kill Tisdale, and this time there'd be no masking his face behind any bandanna.

Somewhere ahead of him on the main road traveled John Tisdale, and on the dying vestiges of the last Monday of December. Tisdale's drunken spree had kept him in Buffalo when he could have made it home by Christmas, which left Canton's patience wearing damned thin. This time Canton had packed along a field glass, and coming to an elevation, he used it to pick out the southern reach of the road. Others were using the road, then he sighted in on Tisdale's big lumbering wagon.

"No sense hurrying about it. He'll strike a camp soon's night sets in. Then I'll move in." Instead of his rifle, Frank Canton had packed along a shotgun. A Texan, he had often used it down in that brushy country, and preferred it to a rifle. At close range a shotgun could do a lot of damage, and he planned to be in close when he braced Tisdale.

Later on that day Frank Canton realized he'd lost track of Tisdale's wagon. This could only mean Tisdale had made for shelter, and around sundown he came across wheel markings heading off the main road and veering down a lane, which Canton knew would bring Tisdale to the Cross H ranch. But to make certain, Canton rode on in until he had a view of the buildings and John Tisdale's freight wagon.

"Tomorrow, then, tomorrow you die, dammit."

Just after eight in the morning John Tisdale climbed into his wagon and headed out for the main road. Stacked behind him were sacks of flour and sides of bacon and other provisions, and the Christmas toys the rancher had bought for his children. Stacked up high so everyone could see it was a red sled. The puppy was wrapped up in a coat on the seat next to Tisdale, and the bitch lay curled on the floorboards.

His team of a gray and a brown found it slow going on the upward parts of the road, and as for John Tisdale, there was still in him the fear of being waylaid by Canton. Rarely did he let his anger get the better of him, but when you'd nursed a grudge for so long, anything could happen. Sunk in the seat, he heard another vehicle wheeling in from behind, to find it was mailman Sam Stringer, who had the mail route to the settlements out along Powder River. Tisdale pulled up just short of a sunken draw called Haywood's Gulch, and promptly he asked:

"You catch any glimpse of Frank Canton?"

"Nope, Mr. Tisdale, I sure didn't. But I heard about that little ruckus. You mind taking some mail along."

"Might's well," Tisdale said crossly, "as a few more pounds won't slow me down any."

"Slow you down." Stringer laughed, added, "You're going slow as a turtle now. Obliged, Mr. Tisdale."

Reining his mules into a jiggling canter, from the seat of his buckboard mailman Sam Stringer wondered about that new shotgun of Tisdale's. And Tisdale hadn't acted all that friendly. These were the thoughts accompanying Stringer as he brought the buckboard through the gulch, and again to pull up as did rancher Charlie Basch astride one of his broncs. There was a brief exchange of small talk, Basch checking out the time by Stringer's watch, and they rode on.

The only witness to their brief meeting just south of Haywood's Gulch was the eye of Frank Canton pressed against his field glass. "Awful busy place this morning." The words came out tight-lipped and edgy as Canton got down off his horse about a hundred yards north of the trail and beyond the rim of a small rise. He'd been seen leaving Buffalo, but on the road, he brushed the worry

150

of it aside. Killing Tisdale would be the same as getting rid of a lobo wolf. Besides, if the law stepped in afterward, the association would be there to back him up.

As he walked around the base of the hill, brush tore at his long winter coat. Snow lay about ankle-deep on the rough ground and on brush and the few pines. Moving on in, the place he picked to do the killing was in the gulch, where a clay abutment about his height would conceal him from the road. Beyond this, about a hundred yards, was higher ground and the road. Impatient, and feeling the gritting teeth of the cold winter day, he paced back and forth behind the abutment.

Finally he heard the creaking of Tisdale's wagon as it loomed over the gulch before its driver began braking the wagon toward the bottom of the gulch. Closer came his intended prey, John Tisdale aware only of keeping the horses moving to get his rig out of the gulch where he could rest them on level ground. As the horses began climbing, out from behind the abutment stepped Frank Canton until he was well within shotgun range, Tisdale's exposed back only about twenty feet away and the man unaware of what was about to happen.

He pulled one trigger on his double-barreled shotgun, the pattern of scattering shot just grazing Tisdale's side but knocking loose his six-gun contained in a shoulder sling under his coat and hitting one of the horses in the neck. Canton's second unleashed shotgun shell struck into Tisdale's back and he crumbled onto the toys he was bringing home for his children.

"That should even the score," Canton said as he hurried past the wagon and up to the eastern edge of the gulch. Distantly he could see someone coming in, but with an indifferent shrug Canton went to retrieve his horse, a sorrel he called Old Fred. Riding back to the wagon, he led the team and wagon deeper into the gulch and out of sight of the road. One of the horses kept whickering at the smell of blood coming from its mate, and then Canton pulled out his sidearm, with a single shot for either horse, dropping them in their traces.

"There, that'll be the end of this thing . . . Tisdale."

As he brought his horse around and set a course for Buffalo, the bitch took off running after him, and callously Frank Canton drew down on the dog, with one shot tumbling her over.

Just before noon Frank Canton was back in town and having a drink with folks still celebrating the holidays.

Fourteen

Undersheriffs Roles and Donahue and a local named Tom Gardner found the wagon just where Charlie Basch said it would be, hidden in Haywood's Gulch. Both horses lay dead in their traces, and dismounting, they took a closer look at John Tisdale's body. They found the tracks of the killer and of his horse, the trail it left beelining directly to the north. Shortly afterward the coroner arrived in a buggy, and it was he who discovered something moving under a coat wrapped up on the seat. This proved to be the puppy given to Tisdale by hardware dealer Munkres.

"Where's the sheriff?"

"Red's tied up in court," a deputy replied.

"Should be here," the undertaker groused as he watched the lawmen go about their investigative work. After a few minutes he'd come to the realization that neither of the deputies were much of a hand at figuring out what to do. "One of them should follow those tracks left by the killer's horse," the coroner said. For they were laid out plain in snowy ground being softened as it warmed into the fifties.

Tom Gardner, with a quiet word to the under-taker, mounted up and left to carry word to the foothill settlements. Hard riding brought him to Jack Flagg's place shortly after midnight, where he broke the news about Tisdale. After a brief rest, Gardner was in the saddle again and heading for the Red Fork and the Tisdale ranch. Just before sunrise he rode in, to arouse the wife of the murdered man.

"Got some awful bad news for you, ma'am."

Around noon Tom Gardner and Tisdale's widow and his children had collected with other ranchers and their families at the Flagg ranch. By midafternoon everyone, including the widow, had started for Buffalo.

Already in Buffalo was Charlie Basch, but all he'd told was of finding the dead man's body back there in Haywood's Gulch. Basch knew far more than that, and as he sat eating dinner alone, a drink at his elbow, all he could think about was that it was damned unhealthy coming upon a killer going about his killing business.

What Charlie Basch had seen back there was a team and wagon standing in the road . . . a horseman who he knew right away was Frank Canton . . . Canton bringing the team away from the road and back into the darkness of the gulch. Before this, Charlie Basch had heard the distant booming of a scattergun, not once but twice. Going in for a closer look, he had seen Canton. Next, two more shots from a handgun reverber-ated over to the frightened Charlie Basch. Then, farther away, a third shot for some unaccountable reason, and a last glimpse of Frank Canton making tracks for Buffalo.

"Let them lawmen handle it," he mused

silently, uneasily. But what worried Basch now was that Cross H ramrod Elmer Freeman had overtaken him on the way here, and he had told Freeman the shank of what had happened. He'd let Freeman notify the sheriff's office, just wanted at the moment to get this chowing-down over and head out again.

"I know it was Canton on that Old Fred hoss of his. But neighbor or not, Canton's nobody to mess with. Just leave it lay; yup, keep out of this."

Before the dawning of another day, word had spread throughout Johnson County and beyond about the murder of rancher John Tisdale. This brought Johnny Jones up to Buffalo to search for his brother, Ranger. Five days was a long time for Ranger to be gone, figured Johnny Jones.

In Buffalo he soon learned that Ranger had left with his wagon, and mustering a search party, they began coming along the road to the south, going up into the draws and gullies. That evening wagon tracks brought some of them away from the road again and there in a draw was found the frozen body of Ranger Jones still draped over the wagon seat. That same evening they were back in Buffalo with the news of another murder.

But even while the search party was out looking for Ranger Jones, two men were discussing all that had happened in a downtown law office belonging to Carroll H. Parmelee. As Justice of the Peace here in Buffalo, Parmelee sided with the cattle kings, and he was also an aide-de-camp to Wyoming Governor A. W. Barber.

155

"I killed both of them," Frank Canton admitted.

"By order of the association?"

"They issued it."

"Yes, I can understand why."

"Fred Hesse was there when I gunned down Ranger Jones. But that's just between us. Reason I mentioned this is because there'll probably be witnesses."

"Does Hesse know you're here . . . or that you were going to kill Tisdale?"

"Nope."

"You'll need an alibi."

"That I'll leave in your capable hands, Mr. Parmelee."

"There will be a hearing—over which I'll preside."

"Then Hesse and I have nothing to worry about."

"I don't believe we'll have to drag Hesse into this."

"Whatever suits you."

Parmelee rose and thrust out a soft hand. "Frank, you're doing a good job. Too bad Tisdale had a family. But he was a rustler. Once I tell our people what I want, Mr. Canton, you'll have a damned good alibi."

Pausing, Canton said, "One thing, Charlie Basch came across me out there. But we'll worry about that later." With a finger touching against the brim of his black hat, Frank Canton took his departure.

Several days after Buffalo found out it was confronted with two murders, the truth of what happened was still clouded. It seemed through all of this everyone was more concerned about John Tisdale's killing than of the other rancher, Jones.

Into town came Nate Champion and a lot of his friends, drawn there by the need to seek out the truth or just for the protection the town offered. Slowly Sheriff Red Angus began to piece together what evidence he had, which turned out to be mailman Stringer coming forth to tell of his overtaking Tisdale on that fateful day, and others, Freeman and the housewife who'd seen the man with the handkerchief concealing his face.

Then it came out as to how Charlie Basch had actually seen the killer. Confronted with this by the sheriff, Basch called out the name—Frank Canton. As a result of this, a warrant was issued for Canton's arrest.

Fifteen

The cattle kings raised their glasses to salute Major Frank Wolcott seated at their table in one of the Cheyenne Club's banquet rooms. From their general talk so far they were more than pleased at the recent events up in Johnson County. Wolcott had been assuring them no effort would be spared in the upcoming hearing to be held at Buffalo.

"As you know, Justice of the Peace Parmelee will be presiding over that hearing. So there isn't too much Frank Canton and Hesse have to worry about."

"We certainly hope so, Major Wolcott."

"Canton has witnesses who will testify he never left Buffalo on the day Tisdale was . . . gunned down. I don't know what the fuss is all about up there, gentlemen, as both Tisdale and this Jones were known cattle thieves."

One of the ranchers said dryly, "I've learned through the years a lot of things can go wrong. The fact remains Frank Canton shot those men down in cold blood. By your orders of course, Major Wolcott."

"By order, sir, of the association. We feel it was

159

something that had to be done."

"So," interrupted another rancher, "there's going to be a hearing—all due process of law. What do you hear from our friend in Texas, Wolcott?"

From an inner pocket Wolcott lifted out a telegram which he'd received just that morning. "Pass it around if you will." A triumphant smile held on Wolcott's squarish face even as he used a big fat toothpick to dislodge a piece of chicken from between his teeth.

"So, Tom Smith is coming back from Texas . . ."

"Bringing some gunhands with him."

"The usual run of hardcase?"

"All of these men are former lawmen of one kind or another," responded Wolcott. "I'm to meet up with them in Denver."

"So it begins," a rancher said thoughtfully.

Another said firmly, "For damned sure these rustlers will steal everything we have unless something of this nature isn't undertaken. I agree with Wolcott—we need to raise an army of our own. The U.S. army won't step in . . . so we've got to." He raised his glass again. "To the courageous Major Wolcott."

Across the wide expanse of Cheyenne settling in for the night, another telegram had been received by *Chicago Gazette* reporter James Haskins. It spelled out orders for him to head up to Buffalo and find out more about the recent murders. Of course Jim Haskins would go, as Corrie Middleton was there, and others he'd come to know. Pausing in the midst of packing some clothes, he said idly:

160

"You do miss her, Mr. Haskins."

Here in Cheyenne he had gotten tired of covering the activities of the stockmen's association and the cattle kings, had fired off a letter to Chicago expressing his desire to return. That had been a week ago. Now he had orders to the contrary.

Pulling out his watch, he realized it was a little early to be turning in. And perhaps a drink or two would serve to drive away some of the encroaching chill of this wintry night when he did climb into bed. He donned his overcoat and hat and left his room to start down the staircase, only to find crossing the lobby toward him a telegraph clerk who'd been supplying him, but at considerable cost, copies of telegrams received by Major Frank Wolcott.

"This is what you've been waiting for, Mr. Haskins. No . . . no . . . this one'll cost you a double eagle." He held out a suggestive hand.

"That's a lot of money."

The clerk was a small, humpbacked man in his late forties, dressed in a shapeless suit under a plaid coat, and he looked about furtively. "If Wolcott's boys find out I've been doing this . . ."

With some reluctance Jim Haskins dropped silvery coin into the man's hand in exchange for a yellow envelope. While the telegraph clerk hurried past the staircase to head for a back door, Haskins sat down on an overstuffed chair in the lobby. As he'd expected, the telegram, when he removed it from the envelope, was addressed to Major Frank Wolcott, and below this a cryptic message; arriving in Denver on or about the fifteenth. There were just some initials below that, and Haskins murmured:

"T . . . S?" He knew that the association had

sent one of their stock detectives down to Texas. Could it be to recruit some gunhands for this army that was supposed to invade Johnson County?

Jim Haskins mulled over other things he had been able to nose out about Major Wolcott's activities in the past month, such as his sending rancher Van Tassel off into Colorado to buy horses, most certainly a move made to quell any questions that would be asked if some of the cattle kings started to bring in their horses before spring roundup. Here in Cheyenne had come a shipment of varying weapons, to be bought by Wolcott's henchmen. And what about the orders issued recently by the governor, in which he had ordered the state militia not to heed the call of local authorities in case of an invasion. Finally, but so far this was only a rumor, arrangements had been made with railroad officials to bring a special train into Cheyenne.

"Horses . . . and they've got weapons too," pondered Jim Haskins. "Now it boils down to manpower." For in the bars of Cheyenne it was common knowledge that though a lot of cattle kings had given money, that was as far as they would go, leaving to Major Wolcott the task of raising his army.

"If so, Wolcott is going to Denver. And so am I."

This would rule out his going to Buffalo. It couldn't be helped as he felt strongly that Major Wolcott was going to Denver to take charge of an army of hired mercenaries. Once this had proved out, he could send a telegram up to Buffalo warning of the impending invasion by the stockmen's association.

In the coming week he kept track of the major's movements about the city. It wasn't until Thursday that shortly after sunup he sighted Major Wolcott with valise in hand departing from his hotel and hopping into a transom hack. Hailing down another cab, Jim Haskins found that Wolcott's vehicle was soon pulling up before the railroad station. But Haskins held to his cab for a moment as three men he recognized as being stock detectives also got aboard the passenger train. As for Haskins, there was barely enough time to purchase a ticket to Denver and dash across the wide expanse of platform to catch the departing train.

Sixteen

A lot of people had come in the night before to acquire lodging in Buffalo. Still others left their homesteads and ranches well before dawn to park their carriages and buggies by the courthouse. Shortly before the hearing was to begin, there wasn't a place to tie up any vehicles or horses. The mood of the crowd was quiet, orderly, the air inside the courtroom filled with a hushed expectancy.

One of those fortunate enough to claim a seat in the courtroom was Nate Champion, whose concerned words traveled only into the ears of Jack Flagg seated to his right. "There's certainly enough evidence against Canton. But I've got this feeling . . ."

"What I don't like, Nate, is Parmelee presiding over this hearing. You know he's been going around town lining up witnesses on Canton's behalf. Seems to me it's a conflict of interest him being Canton's lawyer and also in charge of this hearing. The honorable thing would be for him to step down."

"Honor," came Champion's bitter reply, "is

Parmelee's short suit."

Nate Champion crossed one leg over the other as he took in Sheriff Red Angus and his deputies and the witnesses for the prosecution seated close to the lawmen. There was the mailman Stringer, and Charlie Basch, and the homesteader's wife who'd encountered a masked man, this according to what she'd revealed earlier, on her way in to Buffalo on the day of Tisdale's murder. With them sat rancher Elmer Freeman. Just the testimony of one of these people, Champion figured, should be enough to convict Canton.

It had taken some time to get this hearing going, before which Frank Canton had gone into hiding, and Champion knew that a lot of folks hereabouts had been looking for Canton just to string him up. But Champion knew that if this had happened, they'd be no better'n those cattle kings or their stock detectives. For it had come out that Waggoner had been strung up by detectives employed by the stockmen's association, and there was the Cattle Kate affair.

A door opened and the court clerk came out first to spread herself behind a small table below the wide oaken bench above which big dust-tinted windows let in strands of morning sunlight. The air in the courtroom had a kind of musky odor mingled with some kind of disinfectant which the janitor had used to clean out the big room, a scent that pricked at the nostrils and made a man want to leave. But nobody would be leaving until the Canton hearing was settled. For the moment a lot of folks drew some amusement from the court clerk trying to wedge her big rounded buttocks onto a small wooden chair that creaked as she shifted about, shuffling papers and trying to look important. Though every so often those seated on that side would cast irritated eyes at two windows that had been left open to let in cold wintry air in an attempt to get rid of the offensive odors. Finally a big hulking muleskinner rose and slammed both windows down, this drawing from the court clerk a disapproving glance.

"When's it—"

Jack Flagg's muttered complaint to Champion was cut off when the bailiff, salty old Ambrose Kiley, a holstered gun adorning his right hip and just a lanky man seeming to be shortening up with age, emerged from the judge's chamber and announced in that flat monotone of his:

"All rise for the honorable Carroll H. Parmelee."

Benches creaked and boots scraped against floorboards and a few hacked to clear their throats as Parmelee swept out of his chambers. He hadn't bothered with this nonsense of wearing a black robe but had on a black claw-hammer coat and gray flannel trousers cuffing over black cowboy boots. He didn't bother to smile, as was his way. Now he began prattling on as to the reason for this hearing even as he gaveled everyone to reclaim their seats.

Now Nate Champion took in the witnesses for the defense and Frank Canton seated among his cronies. All of them were business and professional people of Buffalo, and Champion knew, identified with the cattlemen's party. About all they could do was to testify to Canton's character, but he felt it was more than that, and speculating worry ran tracks across his face.

His introductory ramblings over, Parmelee laid smug eyes on Sheriff Red Angus. "Red, you understand this is only a hearing . . . being held to determine if a jury trial should be held in the matter of . . . yes, Mr. Frank Canton versus the State of Wyoming. You may proceed."

"I'll call up my deputies first." And the sheriff did, and both of them related of how they had found John Tisdale's body out in Haywood's Gulch. Further testimony illicited from them by Angus revealed that one of the deputies, Donohue, had followed tracks left by the killer for about two miles before turning around and rejoining the others at Haywood's Gulch.

"Only two miles," said Parmelee. "By now it's warmed up enough for those tracks to be wiped out, I assume."

"Guess so," muttered Red Angus. "Stringer, you was out there. Step up here to the witness stand and give us a rundown on that."

The words of Sam Stringer were as unchanged as when he'd first given his statement to the sheriff, and next came Elmer Freeman to add what he knew.

Nate Champion whispered to Flagg as Freeman returned to his seat back among the benches, "Charlie Basch is next. You heard how he's been hiding out so's not to run into friends of Canton. Parmelee's sure to browbeat Charlie once he's up there." Champion stole a glance at Frank Canton, whose face seemed set in passive lines but there was no mistaking the cold glint in those yellowish eyes.

"So, Charlie," the sheriff said to Basch as he settled uneasily onto the seat next to the high bench of Parmelee's, "what you told my office before has been duly recorded. But the court wants to hear it again."

"Yup," Basch said nervously, and with a hasty glance Canton's way, "why I'm here."

"I'm just going to"—Sheriff Red Angus held papers detailing the testimony of Charlie Basch at the coroner's inquest—"start out with . . . yeah, Charlie, the horse, at the inquest you stated you wasn't able to recognize it as belonging to Canton."

"No, I did recognize the horse, sheriff. It was Canton's, awright, that Old Fred of his—blazed face and white stockings on its hind legs, yessirree it was Canton's."

"Mr. Basch," cut in Parmelee, "are you refuting your earlier testimony?"

"Just . . . just clearing the air is all."

"Then you lied before . . . and could be lying now."

"Mr. Parmelee," muttered Angus, "this is a duly sworn witness . . . and he's got more to say."

"The truth, I hope." Carroll Parmelee settled back on his high bench and cast a pained look at Frank Canton.

"Charlie, you'll swear to this?"

"Yup, sheriff, I'm willing to swear to it now."

"Describe the man riding that horse?"

Reluctantly the man on the witness stand told of seeing a man wearing a drab-colored overcoat and black hat creased down the middle, and with a scarf wrapped around the lower portion of his face.

"You were some distance away, Charlie . . ."

"Maybe half a hundred yards, sheriff. Man I saw had a black hat doubled down on top; no question about that."

"You held back? Why didn't you ride on in?"

"That hombre was fisting a six-gun. Wasn't

about to ride in on nobody holding a gun and ready to use it."

"Mr. Parmelee, you want to ask any questions?"

"I certainly do, sheriff." Justice of the Peace Parmelee's withering cross-examination of this latest testimony by Charlie Basch brought about a lot of wavering and confused answers.

"You just said you weren't sure if it was Canton at all, Basch."

"Thought it was," he said uncertainly.

Disdainfully Parmelee said, "You may step down. Well, it's about noon. We'll recess until one o'clock." His banging gavel brought everyone moving toward the exits.

It was at the Senate Saloon that Nate Champion and Jack Flagg and others siding with them arrived to partake of a free lunch spread out on one of the tables, with hard coin fetching them drinks. Johnny Jones, whose brother had also been murdered, said:

"Seems everyone's forgotten about Ranger."

"One hearing at a time, Johnny," said Flagg. "It's damned obvious what Parmelee is doing."

"He sure cut Basch to ribbons. And where's Fred Hesse, I haven't seen him around for some time."

"Yeah, charges should have been brought against Hesse too."

Nate Champion said, "Canton knows that if he gets out of this, I'll be out gunning for him."

Leaning closer, Flagg said, "Just between us, Nate, but if that happens, Canton will have a hard time leaving town . . . as a lot of his enemies are keeping a close watch on him."

"Stringing up Canton won't solve anything," responded Champion. "The man's got to own up to what he did."

"Unlikely to happen."

"This afternoon, Canton takes the stand. After what happened this morning, Jack, I don't think our honorable sheriff is up to the job of getting the truth out of Canton. I'm afraid of what's going to happen . . . for if Canton gets let off, this town'll explode for sure."

"No, your honor, on the day that John Tisdale was murdered, I never left the city of Buffalo."

"Perhaps, Mr. Canton, you loaned your horse to someone."

"Of course not—and I always keep the stable locked." With this statement Frank Canton returned the smile of the justice of the peace, as Canton added, "As for my whereabouts that morning, I've asked some very reputable citizens of Buffalo to testify on my behalf."

"Good, Frank . . . ah, Mr. Canton," beamed Parmelee. He excused Canton from the witness stand. He disregarded the muttered bursts of anger coming from some of those seated in the courtroom as Frank Canton sought another seat. The first witness to come forward on Canton's behalf was druggist Eggleston.

"Why, sure, Frank and some of his friends dropped into my drugstore around eight-thirty. As a matter of fact"—Eggleston rummaged around in his coat pocket and came up with a slip of paper— "I filled this prescription for Mr. Canton's wife; she's got the gout, you know."

As one and then another witness came forward to add their testimony to bolster what the others had stated, that Frank Canton had never left Buffalo on the morning of the Tisdale murder, there rippled throughout the courtroom mutterings of anger and disbelief. Throughout all of this, Sheriff Red Angus was there to cross-examine each of Canton's witnesses. He could shake nary a word spoken by these men, a doctor, some cattlemen, the steward of the local social club, and others.

As for Nate Champion, as evening shadows closed about the courthouse, most of his burning anger was for the shameful way the justice of the peace was conducting the hearing. Not only was he interrupting the questions being asked by the sheriff of Johnson County but somehow backing up the testimony of Canton's friendly witnesses.

"There's gonna be blood on the moon," uttered Champion in a quiet aside to Jack Flagg. "Canton's guilty and everyone here knows it."

Suddenly Parmelee was rapping his gavel for order as some of the crowd began shoving to their feet to surge toward the doors. "Order, let's have order in here. There's no way . . . there's no way we can wrap this thing up tonight, so—"

Sheriff Red Angus said loudly, "I want this hearing continued tomorrow, Parmelee. Dammit, you lined up all of these witnesses for the accused . . . for Canton. I want an equal chance to bring in some rebuttal witnesses, for there's others who saw Canton leave town."

"This hearing is adjourned." Parmelee hurried to the door directly behind the bench and held it open as Canton and some of the witnesses rushed in there. The bailiff remained in the courtroom to prevent anyone from entering the judge's chambers.

"It shouldn't have taken this long," flared Jack Flagg. "What a shameful exhibition by that damned Parmelee."

"What now, Jack? Do we try and get at Canton?"

"Easy with that kind of talk," broke in Champion. "This isn't over with."

But what happened the following morning proved Nate Champion to have judged wrongly, for at nine o'clock Justice of the Peace Parmelee announced in the courtroom that he found the defendant, Frank Canton, innocent of the charge of first-degree murder. Even in Cheyenne the decision was greeted with derision as was the conduct of Carroll Parmelee.

A few days later Canton and Fred Hesse made a break for Gillette, some hundred miles away, to be chased by seven men determined to see that justice was done. But mounted on superior horses Canton and Hesse made it to their destination, and from there fled the state of Wyoming.

While just before leaving Buffalo to head back to his ranch, Nate Champion uttered these warning words:

"They've made a mockery of the law, these lying cattle kings and their henchmen. What next? Watch your backsides is all I can say."

Seventeen

When James Haskins detrained from a Denver Pacific passenger car, it was to find the city of Denver gripped by a snowstorm. He'd lingered in the car until the Wolcott party had gone by on the bustling platform, then trailed them outside in a covered hack. He soon found his hack pulling up just short of the Golden Hotel on Denver's prestigious Federal Boulevard. He watched as Major Wolcott and the others entered the hotel, knew that he didn't want to risk staying there, and asked the driver to take him to a nearby hotel.

"Isn't this the twelfth?" Haskins commented.

"Has been all day, mister."

"Does it snow this way all the time?"

"Get some fierce winds in these parts, and a lot of snow." The driver frowned as he took in his passenger's Western clothing. "You must have just moved out here as that's a Midwestern slant to your words."

"From Chicago," he ventured, as the driver brought his hack away from the curbing to head north on the boulevard. Another block and he rounded a corner to give Jim Haskins a closer look

175

at the capitol building's golden dome.

Along the way he checked on what money he had left in his wallet, and said worriedly, "Fifty dollars won't carry me too far." The main thrust of his worry was of lingering on here in Denver, which would necessitate his newspaper wiring him more money, or discovering that the telegram received by Major Wolcott was innocuous in nature. But during the hundred-mile train ride from Cheyenne he'd figured out the telegram had been sent by Tom Smith, an association detective who'd departed over a month ago for Texas.

"Probably coming in with a bunch of gunfighters."

Early the next morning Jim Haskins found that it had stopped snowing though snow had blocked a lot of streets as he entered a haberdashery just up-street from his hotel, The Westerner. After a change of clothing back in his room, he left to walk the three blocks to Major Wolcott's hotel. The hotel was a four-story brick building reaching out for about half a block down Federal Boulevard. His inquiry at the spacious desk in the lobby revealed that Major Wolcott was in a second-floor suite. Barely had he settled onto a chair in the lobby and reached for a copy of the *Rocky Mountain News* when he realized Wolcott's henchmen were coming down the staircase, to head out onto the boulevard and hail down a hack.

Tossing the newspaper aside, Jim Haskins had a hesitant scowl on his face as he hurried over to the revolving doors and looked outside. Either they were heading someplace for breakfast or, as he suspected, were doing some chore for the major. A glance back at a wall clock told him it was going on nine-thirty. Wolcott could be down at any moment to go with the stock detectives or Haskins concluded hastily, the major might stay in his suite. Hurrying outside, he crossed the sidewalk to a hack just pulling up to the curbing.

When the hack in front began wending its way down a narrow street toward Union Station, it gave the man following it the impression that the stock detectives were merely going to catch a train back to Cheyenne. Instead the leading hack rolled past the station and passed along the ribbon of steely tracks comprising the vast railroad yard.

"Hold up," Haskins warned his driver as the other hack pulled up by a long string of cattle cars idling on a siding. Then Haskins handed the driver his fare and got out to trudge through the newly fallen snow toward the three men cutting around behind the cars. "Jim Elliott's one of them; I'll never forget what he did to me up at Buffalo."

The wind slammed at Jim Haskins when he came around the cattle cars to find other cars scattered about on the tracks running north-south. When the men ahead of him suddenly veered over to a short string of cars, one a passenger car and the others flat and freight cars, he pulled up short to watch from the end of a freight car. From his vantage point he had little difficulty recognizing that the flat cars carried wagons covered by large green tarpaulins; the freight cars though seemingly empty could carry horses; all the shades were pulled down on the windows of the passenger car. In about a half-hour Elliott and his companions emerged from the passenger car and began moving back through the railroad yard.

"All those cars need now," pondered Haskins as he headed over, "is a locomotive hooked to them."

He tried to enter the passenger car, only to discover that the doors at both ends were locked. Passing back, he climbed up on the first flat car. Under the tarpaulins, he found, were horse-drawn commissary wagons. Making his way back to the other flat car, curiosity as to the presence of only one vehicle on it brought him poking around under the covering tarpaulin.

"An ambulance?" He pushed out from under the tarpaulin and away from the wind. "So there is going to be an invasion?" The next question troubling Haskins was just how large an army Major Wolcott and Secretary Ijams had been able to muster. Jumping down, he headed back through the endless tracks toward Union Station.

Feeling the biting teeth of the blustery day, he went into the station and found the large restaurant, there to drive the chill away with a cup of coffee. Here he began sorting out of his thoughts the seeds of a newspaper story. But in so doing he tried to match his ideas of what to do with those of Major Wolcott's. First the train with the hired gunhands would have to be brought down in secret to Cheyenne, and from there it most certainly was still a considerable distance to Johnson County. Though winter was giving way to the balmier days of early spring, out here storms would often hit without warning. But he doubted that a storm or anything else was going to hold back the venging hand of Major Wolcott.

"Most any day now they'll pull out for Cheyenne. But I've got to be sure about Wolcott hiring outsiders to do his killing work."

They came in that weekend, Tom Smith and around twenty hired guns. Major Wolcott was

178

waiting at Union Station when the Denver and Rio Grande train chugged in, and Wolcott wasted little time in ushering everyone through the railroad yard to another train waiting back on a siding.

The only other person aware of those gunfighters coming into Denver was Jim Haskins, who'd earlier this Saturday morning gone over to find a locomotive being hooked to Major Wolcott's secret war train. Quickly he had found a telegraph office and sent a wire up to Buffalo to warn of the major's intentions.

Slipping between two boxcars coupled together, Haskins took in the Texans scrambling aboard the passenger car, and by his reckoning there were twenty-three men including Wolcott. As the engine sat there throwing out impatient gusts of coal smoke, some of the stock detectives went back along the cars checking out ropes, tying down tarpaulins, and looking for stowaways.

"They'll pick up more men once they reach Cheyenne," Haskins thought. "But at least now I know the stockmen's association has violated the laws of Wyoming by bringing in outsiders. Once my editor reads my story, he'll realize why I didn't go up to Buffalo. And I'll send another wire up to Buffalo warning them about these Texans . . ."

A scraping sound alerted Jim Haskins that he'd been discovered, and he started to spin around, only to have stock detective Joe Elliott pull the trigger on his six-gun.

"Elliott, you—" Jim Haskins exclaimed even as something slammed into his side. Desperately he threw himself out from between the boxcars, with another bullet from Joe Elliott's gun ricocheting off a steel railing. Regaining his feet, Jim Haskins

179

broke away, only to have another gunman appear. Haskins simply threw himself under the boxcar, scrambled to the other side, and started running at a hobbling gait toward another long line of railroad cars. His assailants came around the boxcars and threw some more bullets after Haskins, then they broke away when their prey vanished behind a freight train ghosting into the yard.

"He's hit."

"I know," affirmed Ben Morrison.

"It was that meddling reporter. But I reckon he won't bother us again." Both men scrambled aboard the train beginning to roll to the north.

Weakened by the bullet that had penetrated deep into his side, Jim Haskins could barely make out the looming walls of Union Station just a short distance away. He brought a bloodied hand away from his side as he called out to some people just alighting from a carriage.

"Please, I . . ."

Suddenly the cinder-littered ground between a row of rails came up to slam into his face and everything faded away.

"What's he doing out here?"

"I don't know . . . but he's still alive."

"Hurry or we'll miss our train."

"Can't leave him here, though I doubt he'll pull through. Easy now, we'll carry him into Union Station as they'll know what to do."

Eighteen

A protesting sob burst from the lips of Corrie Middleton as she struggled to cast away her troubling dream. Somehow she managed to sit up in bed and blink away the last shreds of sleep.

". . . men with guns . . . Jim Haskins . . . something's happened to him."

Swinging her legs to the floor, she brought both hands to her face to brush the long strands of hair away, still troubled by her dream, the dread in her that something had really happened to Jim. She stared at rosy light just beginning to seep into her bedroom, realized it would be impossible to go back to sleep, and lithely she pulled up from the bed, Corrie's lissome form enhancing the tight-fitting nightgown.

"Yes," came another thought, "Nate would be in town today." Earlier in the week she'd received a letter from Nate Champion, that he wanted to see her. He'd never written to her before, had in the last few weeks made no attempt to come over.

"My father's doings," she said irritably as a youthful stride brought her into the bathroom, where she set about starting a fire in the small stove. After it had flamed up, she began to heat water for her morning bath.

Still gripped by the details of her dream, Corrie Middleton knew she had strong feelings for Jim, as she still retained for Nate Champion. Jim Haskins had a more serious nature, a crusader of sorts if you will, a young man whose thirst for the truth could bring him harm. Much to her delight, her father liked Jim, but now Jim Haskins was gone.

"Gal, do you love him?" That question ran around in Corrie's mind as she poured hot water into the round metal bathtub. Removing her nightgown, she eased into the water to let its warmth chase away the tingling of the cold morning air. In a way, she did. And that he loved her was fairly evident from the way he acted when they were together.

Nate Champion, on the other hand, brought with him visions of high skies and mountain vistas and that charming way Nate had of making her feel just right. At first she hadn't been able to quite comprehend why anyone would bear a grudge against Nate, as the cattle kings surely did. But after this first summer here in Buffalo, she came to realize it wasn't just Nate Champion, but all the homesteaders, the small ranchers, even some of the businessmen and duly elected officials, who shared in this aura of distrust of the big ranchers and their stockmen's association.

Nate's letter had asked her to meet him out by that big oak tree just west of Carlin's livery stable, and she assumed they would be going for a buggy ride, which would elicit some excuse she'd have to give her father for missing supper. Nate was also, she felt with a certain heaviness of heart, going to ask her to become his wife. Perhaps if she failed to show up, Nate Champion would realize it wasn't meant to be.

"No, I owe him that," came her demurred answer. "And . . . and Jim . . . is he in trouble?"

Another resident of Buffalo was also experiencing a growing premonition of unease, but for Sheriff Red Angus it was a firm belief that before long his town was going to be torn apart. Angus hadn't even bothered to stop at the Germania House for his usual breakfast of steak and eggs, had instead trudged right to his office. Whereupon Sheriff Angus had stoked the fire to get the coffeepot heated, and then opened his safe.

The coffee he was sipping at the moment was as bitter as his feelings over what lay on his desk. There were a lot hereabouts who'd stated publicly that Sheriff Angus and his deputies had bungled the investigation involving the murder of John Tisdale, that he shouldn't have waited around but gotten right to the business of arresting Frank Canton. But Canton had fled, and what Red Angus was staring at over the rim of his tin cup was the two boxes of shotgun shells found in Tisdale's wagon. There was little question but that they'd been tampered with.

Quietly he had tracked down just where they'd been purchased by John Tisdale, this along with a shotgun just before Tisdale had set out for his ranch.

"At George Munkres Hardware Store."

John Tisdale, Sheriff Angus had found out from most everyone in town, had been on a binge. Before this, Tisdale had buffaloed Canton over at a saloon, and Canton had run out the back door.

Canton had been publicly humiliated, and realizing this, John Tisdale had feared that once he struck out for his ranch, he might be ambushed. He had, and no question but by Frank Canton. "But this, this"—angrily Sheriff Red Angus stared at the incriminating boxes of shotgun shells—"for Munkres to do this. The cowardly cur is just as guilty."

Before he was elected to the office of sheriff, Red Angus had known little about the law. But he'd learned how hard it was to enforce the law up here. Some called him buffoon, that he'd got elected only because old barfly friends and hardcases that frequented his saloon had voted him into office. He'd learned, too, that the badge pinned to his shirt made him feel more of a man.

Now here he was, poised on the horns of a dilemma, as Sheriff Red Angus knew that if word got out about how George Munkres had tampered with these shells, the odds were that Munkres would be gunned down. Further, he could present this evidence to Justice of the Peace C. H. Parmelee. That, he knew, would be the last anyone would ever see of these shotgun shells.

Another thing rankling Red Angus was the letter received by him a few weeks ago from a friend down in Cheyenne. It had pretty much spelled out that he and other officials up here were on a stockmen's association death list.

"But who are the ones handing out death," he declared angrily. "The ones breaking the law and getting away with it. Canton and those damned stock detectives . . . and those ranchers down in the Sweetwater."

He set his cup down hard, and coffee spilled over his cluttered desk. Shoving his chair back, Red

Angus stepped over and placed one box of shells in his safe. Then jamming his hat on his thinning reddish hair and picking up the other box of shotgun shells, he stalked outside and veered upstreet toward Munkres Hardware Store. He took in other business places run by men who'd testified on Frank Canton's behalf at that hearing, the Eggleston Drugstore, Conrad's Mercantile Store, the blacksmith shop, and George Munkres had also told of seeing Canton around ten o'clock on the morning John Tisdale had been murdered. His anger swelling to cloud his thoughts, Sheriff Angus knew without question but that he was going to request a grand jury to be impaneled. Canton's cutting out of here was the same as Canton admitting that he'd killed Tisdale. He knew that without Frank Canton to back them up, those lying witnesses would change their stories.

He reached the hardware store just as one of the clerks was unlocking the front door. And Red Angus shouldered inside to discover to his surprise that other clerks were stowing merchandise in packing crates and that a lot of shelves had been emptied, but of George Munkres there was no sign.

Noticing the wondering grimace on the sheriff's face, one of the clerks said, "I'm sorry to say Mr. Munkres is selling out."

"Appears that way," he said acidly. "Just where is Munkres?"

"At his home, I assume, packing up his furniture. I believe he intends to move back East." The clerk dropped his eyes to the box of shotgun shells. "Did you want some more shells, sheriff?"

"Not the way Munkres sells them." Hesitating, and anger tightening the lines of his face, Red

Angus realized that the hardware dealer was running scared, and that it would serve no purpose in telling these clerks what the man they worked for had done to the shells sold to John Tisdale.

Sheriff Angus went out the front door and along the boardwalk to pause by the alleyway passing along the south wall of Munkres Hardware Store. He could go over and brace George Munkres, make the man confess to what he'd done. Or even throw Munkres in jail for a few days.

"But there's no way Munkres is gonna forget what he did . . . or that he's partly responsible for what happened to Tisdale. Yup, let Munkres live with his nightmares the rest of his life."

Passing into the alley, Red Angus dropped the box of shotgun shells into a trash barrel, would keep the other box in his safe as evidence just in case Frank Canton was brought to trial. Then, dammit, Munkres would be brought back to testify against Canton.

"And I promise that day is gonna come."

Her petticoats rustling against her legs, Corrie Middleton quickened her stride when she rounded the corner of a building to find that Nate Champion was waiting under the oak tree. Clambering down from the buggy seat, Nate's smile took in Corrie's flushed face and the tentative smile as he said:

"Hi, it's been some time."

"A long time," she agreed as he helped her onto the seat, then he went around and climbed in beside Corrie, picking up the reins and heading westerly out of Buffalo.

Nate Champion brought his rig over the river

bridge and let the pair of horses labor up the graded road which would eventually end at Fort McKinney. Though the sun had passed behind the mountain before them, spreading out around them and from higher up came a hazy alpenglow which would hold upon the lower reaches they were on for several more hours, and even so, they passed through lengthening shadows of a warm day. Except for those first words of greeting, they'd refrained from further talk. There was, she'd noticed, in the back of the buggy a picnic basket and a woolen blanket folded beside it, and also in Corrie Middleton was a worried quickening of breath, for she felt this would turn out to be more than a sharing of a picnic lunch in some secluded spot.

"Ah, Nate, how is your ranch going?"

"It's there," he said lamely. "Trouble a lot of us are having is finding a place to sell our cattle. Seems"—his voice hardened—"we're being frozen out."

"I'm sorry to hear that."

"Not your worry, Corrie," he replied around an easy smile as he veered away from the road and under a stand of pine trees. Reining up, his smile holding, Nate added, "I heard that newspaperman fella, Haskins, left town."

"Yes, he . . . Jim's editor sent him down to Cheyenne."

"You know, Jim Haskins had more than most around here . . . in that he was an honest man. An' I reckon too honest to suit certain folks in these parts."

Though he hadn't said it, Corrie knew that Nate Champion was referring to the not too long ago time when Jim Haskins had been beaten up by those stock detectives. And seated close to Nate on the buggy seat, she could feel the magnetic pulling of his smiling eyes, felt stirring in her thoughts of how it had been before for them. That Nate Champion was a handsome man she couldn't deny. Then he jumped down to tie up the reins.

After the blanket had been laid out among the pine trees and the picnic basket nestled between Corrie and Nate, they settled their eyes upon the town spread out below and beyond Buffalo to the sweeping vista of the high plains. Despite the serenity of the moment, Corrie could sense a certain tenseness about the man she was with, in the way he moved and in the constant probing of his eyes to nearby places being shadowed by twilight. This brought to mind some unpleasant thoughts her father had expressed about Nate just the other day. After all, she felt, if Nate was going to ask for her hand in marriage, there mustn't be any secrets between them.

"Nate, I must know . . . I mean there are a lot of things being said about you."

"Don't I know," he said bitterly.

"Do you . . . are you one . . . oh, Nate, I . . ."

"Am I a rustler, outlaw, highwayman?"

"Do you belong to the Red Sash gang?"

Instantly his dark eyes flicked to Corrie's, and in them was a certain probing coldness. The outlaw band just mentioned by Corrie Middleton had taken to wearing a red sash around the waist as a badge of membership, and now Nate Champion gestured toward his gunbelt.

"It appears I'm not wearing one of them red sashes."

"No," she said quickly, "You're not."

"Corrie, I . . . I . . ."

"I know, Nate, you asked me out here . . . wanting to marry me."

"Never could slip anything by you, I reckon. And I reckon it just won't take . . . us, Corrie."

Blinking back her tears, Corrie said softly, "Oh, Nate, there's so much hatred out here . . . so much that isn't right."

Through a forced smile he said, "Maybe time will heal all of this—make things right between us. Reckon I'll take you back to town, Corrie Middleton. You know I love you . . . so let's leave it at that for now."

Folks had gotten to calling it Joe DeBarthe's Buffalo, with the editor of the *Buffalo Bulletin* taking considerable pride in this singular distinction, as his newspaper was always lauding a place which he had first seen only two short years ago.

As was his habit of late, Joe DeBarthe was still hunkered over his desk at the newspaper office, the coal oil lamps turned up high, the brow of the editor furrowed to show his growing concern over recent events. Hearing a clatter in the street, he went to the window, and yawning wearily, he watched a buggy rumble by.

"That's Champion . . . Nate Champion . . . and the Middleton girl. Used to see a lot of them together, but her pa . . ." More than once he'd overheard Corrie's father deriding Champion and his friends. "Nate a rustler?" DeBarthe mused. "Don't know, but I'm no saint either."

Turning back to his desk, he picked up the whiskey bottle reposing on a wooden file cabinet and claimed his swivel chair again. These long hours had brought about a loss of weight, as had his not eating regular meals. But zealously Joe DeBarthe had kept writing editorials slanted to show the town he loved in a more favorable light. Despite his efforts, some businessmen were pulling out, and there was no question that the economy had fallen on hard times.

What Joe DeBarthe, and many others, couldn't flee from was how John Tisdale had been found dead, sprawled among the Christmas toys he'd intended to bring home to his children. Or how Ranger Jones had looked, a grimace of death affixed to his face and his bloodstained hair frozen to the buggy seat.

Newspapers such as the *Billings Gazette* had predicted that with the coming of spring the invaders would be going after the rustlers infesting Wyoming.

"Well, spring's settling in early this year," he pondered, "and as yet nothing has happened."

After sipping from the bottle, he set it aside and scratched at his tangled mess of untidy hair while contemplating an editorial he was readying for tomorrow's issue of the *Buffalo Bulletin*. It was in DeBarthe's scrawling longhand, with words scratched out and others added, and he realized with a grim certainty that once it hit the streets, it would further enrage the cattle kings. But as Joe DeBarthe had often said to his friends, and what he murmured now:

"I'm in too deep with all of this to back out now."

Now with a final flourish, he ended his editorial:

Certain paid lickspittles who claim to represent all the virtue and honesty in John-

190

son County have been writing lies to the out-side world about the thieves in this locality. No man who has not sanctioned murder has escaped the calumnies of these vipers. They have even written notes of warning to each other, taken them down to Cheyenne and cried: "See what I have received through the mails."

The reign of terror they yell about rages in their own breasts. The only thing they have to fear are the ghosts of the men who have been murdered. But this fear has grown to such proportions that they see daggers in the eyes of every man who is not numbered in their coterie.

"There," said editor Joe DeBarthe, "that should stir up things, but so help me it's the Gospel. Read some of them stories put out by that reporter from Chicago, that James Haskins, and he pulls no punches." He picked up the bottle and took a healthy swig of corn whiskey. "To you, Mr. Haskins, a truly honest man."

Then he turned out the lamps and locked the door in leaving, beginning a lonely walk to his house and a cold supper, but packing the whiskey bottle and in step with the ghosts of those who'd been murdered.

Nineteen

Until five years ago Will Castleman had ranched up around Powder River. Then in trying to break a wild horse, he sustained a crippling injury to his left arm, and it was either have it amputated or see him die. He hung on for a while, then sold out and brought his family down here to Cheyenne. But Will Castleman still kept in touch with a lot of old friends living up in Johnson County and in Buffalo.

Down here in Cheyenne what he resented most was the one-sided attitude of the cattle kings and the stockmen's association, and all the lies the newspapers hereabouts were telling about the rustling situation. Ever since Will Castleman had picked up rumors about the death list issued by Major Frank Wolcott, there'd been a few letters to Sheriff Red Angus, with Castleman keeping tabs on the three men ruling the stockmen's associations and the comings and goings at the Cheyenne Club.

He had picked up on Major Wolcott striking out for Denver, and Secretary Ijams leaving some time ago for places farther west. Right at this moment he knew that around fifty head of horses brought in from Colorado were being branded down at holding pens in the railroad yard. Wagons loaded with supplies were also down there, but guards posted around the pens had kept him from getting a closer look.

"And that downtown gun store," he remarked dryly, "it's sure been doing a land office business selling rifles to cronies of Major Wolcott's. This is the wrong time of year for elk or antelope hunting."

Will Castleman had a chiseled, leonine face with deep creases caused by years of ranching. Despite his missing left arm, he walked more like a cavalryman than someone having spent a lot of time saddlebound. The silvery hair under the low-crowned hat was neatly groomed, enhancing Castleman's weathered skin, and he had clear, China blue eyes which could go cold at an affront or flash when he smiled. Just fifty, he had on a cattleman's leather coat and creased trousers and he still couldn't keep from wearing spurs attached to his Justins. Around Cheyenne he was treated with considerable respect, though Will Castleman didn't attend a lot of social affairs and kept how he felt to himself. He knew a lot of the cattle kings, but didn't mingle with them, and had declined invitations to be a guest at their club.

One of his favorite pastimes was walking the streets of this pleasant city. And when he did, there was always a friendly nod to panhandlers or drifters, or friends he'd acquired. Today Will Castleman's measured strides took him past the new capitol building crowned by a golden dome, and farther on into a smoke shop. He laid out coin for a pouch of pipe tobacco, then went outside to stand under the shading awning. Tamping tobacco into the bowl of his briar pipe, he fastened his eyes downstreet on the Chandler Hotel.

"Two who'd fled from Johnson County are lodged there."

He still found it hard to believe that Frank Canton and Fred Hesse, those involved in the killings at Buffalo, had dared to venture back to Wyoming. And further troubling Will Castleman was that Canton had been given his old job back as stock detective. This had been detailed to him just last night by one of the bartenders serving drinks over at the Cheyenne Club. Canton's being here only firmed up his opinion that an invasion of Johnson County was imminent.

"According to the brag of a lot of cattle kings, they'd be part of that invasion force. But I wonder . . ."

Mostly they were honest men caught up in the rustling hysteria, that anyplace up around the Big Horns you turn a rock over, there'd be a rustler or outlaw under it. Hammering away at the ranchers with inflaming words had been Ijams and Wolcott. One, Ijams, in Will Castleman's scornful opinion, was a jabbering idiot, and then you had Major Frank Wolcott, a vainglorious fool. Here you had Wolcott, with creditors filing to take away his ranch, and who'd had a multitude of jobs before this, some he'd given up on and two instances where Major Wolcott had been fired for one reason or another. Yet the ranchers were entrusting this man to head up their invasion army.

"Just sucking up to their egos is all Wolcott's been doing."

But despite how Will Castleman felt about the illustrious major, or how the stockmen's association was being run, his immediate concern was the invasion train. And that meant another long walk down to the railroad yard.

Shortly after Major Frank Wolcott's train roared out of Denver, word came to him of the death of *Chicago Gazette* reporter James Haskins. He promptly dismissed the killing as being just another casualty of the rustling war. Along the way, Wolcott made his presence known to the Texans riding with him in the special Pullman car. And when their invasion special finally rolled into Cheyenne that same afternoon, Frank Wolcott knew this was the crowning moment of his life. For there to greet them were a lot of the cattle kings he served, brought into Cheyenne for the annual meeting of the stockmen's association.

Also alighting from a carriage was Secretary Ijams, who greeted Wolcott with an effusive smile and the news that Frank Canton and Fred Hesse were here to become part of the invasion army. This produced a scowl from Wolcott.

"Whose idea was it to bring Canton back here?"

H.B. Ijams knew that in the past Canton and the major had butted heads more than once over association policy, and it was no secret that the cattle kings wanted Canton to take charge of this affair, as Frank Canton was their idea of what a leader should be, a man acquainted with Johnson County as well as having been sheriff up there. Major Wolcott would have none of this, had actually been happy to see the departure of Canton from Wyoming.

"Damn," he snapped, "I should have been consulted about this."

"They didn't even tell me," complained Ijams. "Well, they're expecting us at the Cheyenne Club, a sort of last get-together."

"No," Wolcott said, "I'll stay here and supervise things. As I plan to pull out as soon as everything's loaded on the cars." Struggling to control his anger, he waited until Ijams had left the Pullman car before he turned his attention to the Texans who'd taken all of this in.

"Gentlemen, I insist you keep those blinds down and stay in here. There's plenty of liquor and food. We'll be leaving directly."

Chicago Gazette reporter Jim Haskins wasn't the only one sending a telegram down here, as another wire had arrived from Denver telling of the invasion train. Down along the railroad yard rolled an engine pulling six cars, its passing viewed by yardmen and station loafers, and by Will Castleman lurking at the depot.

Castleman had arrived shortly after eleven-thirty, had taken in the fact that some ranchers were lurking out by the holding pens. Since he came here often, he knew most of the telegraph operators and the ticket agent, but could only illicit a few vague responses to his inquiries about the horses out in those pens.

For a while he watched wranglers herding the horses aboard three stock cars and three new Studebaker wagons stowed onto a flatcar, but of more interest was the arrival of several ranchers— Clarke, Davis, and De Billier, among others— toting bedrolls and rifles and sidearms and clambering into the Pullman car.

"No question but that the invasion is on."

Worriedly Will Castleman went into the depot and sought out the stationmaster, a man who could fill in the missing parts such as when the train would pull out and just how big an army

Major Wolcott had gotten together.

"Mr. Castleman, seems I've seen you around here a lot lately."

"You have," he said none too gently. "And you also know until a few years ago I ranched up there, along Powder River. Which is why I'm here."

"Those horses out there? Why, Castleman, they were brought in from Colorado, as you probably know. Should fetch a high price up here."

"Sir, I respect your loyalty to your railroad. But we both know that train is going to head north—as far as Casper—then those horses will carry men out there up to Johnson County. So a truthful word now just might ease your conscience some."

Under the damning gaze of Will Castleman, the stationmaster filled in a few sketchy details of what the presence of the train here meant, that it would pull out once loading operations were over. "Probably leave in an hour or two," he added reluctantly.

Leaving a curt nod for the stationmaster, Will Castleman left the small office and crossed over to a counter where others were filling out telegram blanks. He scrawled in Sheriff Angus's name at the top and below that a terse message warning that the invasion army was on the way. Then he went over and passed the telegram message to one of the operators he knew, saying:

"Ralph, I'd appreciate your sending that pronto."

"Sure, Mr. Castleman," said the telegraph operator as he was handed the message and two silver dollars. "I'll try to get it sent up there. But I've got to tell you, the line is down."

"Just keep trying."

After Will Castleman had left the depot, Ralph turned to another operator and commented,

"Second message I've gotten like this."

"You mean the one sent down from Denver by that reporter, Haskins."

"Sad thing is neither of these messages will get through. You know what I think . . ."

"That someone cut the wire?"

"Yup, which means the ranchers are playing for keeps. I'll keep trying to get through, but I'll bet a lot of folks are going to get gunned down before that happens."

Better than anyone else, Frank Canton knew the character of the man chosen as commander of the expedition. Which had provoked in him deep moments of concern. It was true Wolcott had his military title and experience thirty years earlier, and his hotheaded way of expressing his opinions. But the way Major Wolcott had of losing his temper coupled with that stubborn nature of his added up to the disturbing fact that he was temperamentally unfit to lead men. It could be also, deliberated Frank Canton, that they just didn't have much use for one another.

"But I'm not putting my name on the line with Wolcott as field commander," he spat out, "and neither should anyone else." Canton smiled at one of the wranglers tending to the horses as he walked his way back along the cars.

It pleased him immensely that he was back in Wyoming, and that it wouldn't be too much longer before he'd be exacting his vengeance against the Johnson County sheriff and others siding with the rustlers. He'd found out that Major Wolcott was supervising the loading of supplies in the baggage car, and clambering up the steps, Canton poked his head into the car. Surveying the stacked boxes of ammunition, he drawled:

"Seems you've got enough shells here to kill the entire population of Wyoming and half of Montana."

"What are you doing here, Canton? Seems to me you were ordered to stay in the Pullman car." Wolcott took out his handkerchief and wiped the sweat from his forehead.

"I want to clear up some things." Entering, Canton allowed a cold smile to appear.

"Are you questioning my authority, my right to be in charge of this . . ."

"Easy, Major, no need to fly off the handle. I just want you to know that some of the ranchers feel we should share responsibility for the expedition. It wouldn't hurt none to share our thoughts on this. No telling what'll happen up there."

"What'll happen is that I'll be issuing any orders concerning our invasion army," raged Major Frank Wolcott. "And now, Canton, I'm ordering you to stay out of my way. Yes, certainly, you have a certain value to us—your expertise with guns and the fact you've been a lawman—but to take charge of things . . . damned absurd, I'd say."

Frank Canton left quietly, but not before letting Wolcott view the sudden chilling of his eyes. Striding back toward the Pullman car, he realized that he should pull out of this thing. For he knew with a fatalistic certainty that Major Wolcott would soon be out of his element.

"There's an omen here," he mused worriedly, "and it doesn't portend well for us. Me, I'll just go along for the ride. But if an opportunity arises, I'm consigning Wolcott to that baggage car."

Twenty

It was a Saturday, almost six months to that day he'd been rushed to a Denver hospital, that James Haskins took a last look at the office he shared with other reporters and then left. Down in front of the *Gazette* building, his raised cane brought a hack pulling to the curbing, and with some difficulty, he eased inside. The bullet wound had left him with some weakness of the spine, and he had thinned out and there was a touch of gray in his hair. And there were the memories.

He stared out at streets festooned with green and red Christmas decorations and bunting and every so often a tree adorned with flickering lights, his thoughts in a kind of suspended reverie. Jim Haskins couldn't rid himself of the memories of all that had happened in Wyoming. Nor, it seemed, did he want to. Perhaps when he'd been recuperating in Denver, he should have written to Corrie Middleton. Instead he had returned to Chicago, since he felt Corrie preferred being a rancher's wife and would marry Nate Champion. Then came the shocking news that Champion and another man had been murdered by the invaders. As had everyone else in Chicago, he'd followed the newspaper stories of all that took place next, the arrest of Major Wolcott's army and their subsequent imprisonment at Fort McKinney, later the forced march as the invaders were brought on foot to Douglas, there to entrain for Cheyenne. What had firmed up Jim Haskins's decision to return to Wyoming was the upcoming trial of the invaders to be held in the First District Court at Cheyenne. And there was Corrie.

This time the train gliding into the railroad yard at Cheyenne was only a passenger train dislodging James Haskins and others and luggage being bundled onto hand carts. He stood there in the cold of a late December morning to savor the dry, crisp air snapping at his face and nose. He couldn't help noticing on the approaches through the city how it had grown, though to him it was still a place of intrigue. And then he was in a hack and heading for his hotel.

In the next few days Jim Haskins discovered to his surprise that the invaders had free access to the streets of Cheyenne, that most of them had taken up residence in their homes or would head out to their ranches. They act, he mused, like righteous knights of yore. Yesterday he'd run into Sheriff Red Angus, here for the trial, and over coffee Angus had told of the bloody end of Nate Champion and Nick Ray.

"It's simply a case of coldblooded murder as they didn't give those boys a chance. Riddled Nate's cabin with bullets before setting it on fire. The bodies were brought back to Buffalo and placed on public exhibition. A grisly sight as all that was left of Nick Ray was his charred and roasted trunk as his head and limbs had been burned away. Champion's body was pierced with bullets."

"Nate wasn't all that bad."

"Bad or good it seemed to make no difference. At the funeral that Methodist sky pilot spouted out that vengeance is the Lord's, that the Lord will repay. Maybe so, and maybe these killers are going to be acquitted."

"That would be a miscarriage of justice."

"Yup, it would be, Mr. Haskins. But legal fees and the other expenses caused by this have cleaned out the coffers of Johnson County. About all we can do now is have our county prosecutor move to have the case dismissed."

Among the other things narrated to him by Sheriff Angus was of the Texans heading for home, and two other invaders, both residents of Wyoming, heading east. That evening Jim Haskins took a stroll past the downtown saloons, where the cattle kings liked to hang out, and then he came upon the Cheyenne Club. From across the street he took in the lights pouring out of the many windows shuttered down for the winter. A lot of carriages were pulling up, and he murmured idly:

"Must be having a party in there. Or it could be that word has gotten out as to the intentions of Johnson County to drop the charges." He felt a sadness settling in, this feeling of despondency. "Have these men no remorse over what happened? No, I suppose not." Then he turned to limp away.

The wintery cold held sway over the dark streets of Cheyenne as Jim Haskins came to Sixteenth

Street. Beckoning to him was a saloon, and beyond that a couple of blocks lay his hotel. He didn't mind the cold as much as in Chicago, where icy winds came off the lake, and Jim Haskins realized since coming back here that being in Wyoming, despite all that had happened, could get to a man. Perhaps it was the openness of the high plains and the people. A man could file on a hunk of land, there were plenty of jobs, and up at Sheridan there was a young woman who brought pain tugging at his heart.

"You'd best write to her," he said chidingly, "as you know blame well you're heading up that way."

Now the need to put his thoughts in a letter to Corrie Middleton brought him traipsing past the saloon, and then something made Jim Haskins break stride. He stopped, turned to look back, keened his ears to the sounds of the city. There, it came again, and off to his left where the alley gaped away, the crunching of a man treading softly over snow. One name came to mind, that of stock detective Joe Elliott. He hadn't brought charges against Elliott, since he still wasn't certain whether Elliott or someone else had shot him back at Denver, but he knew for damned certain that Elliott had been there. And on the way out here from Chicago, Jim Haskins reasoned he would be in danger once these men knew he'd returned.

Quickly he shrank against the building and unpocketed the small handgun he'd taken to packing around. He also had his cane to help ward off any attackers, but that would be of little use against gunmen. Attackers? Perhaps there was only one man in there? Or maybe a stray dog had wandered in to pick at a trash barrel.

When the shots came, they reached out for Jim Haskins from behind, to chip away at the brick wall, and he went into a crouch. The fear of what was happening widening his eyes, he managed to fire a single bullet at a man back at the intersection. And as the ambusher ducked away, Jim Haskins sprang toward the alley and cut away with a couple of random bullets, while the other man in there beat a hasty retreat.

Then it was quiet again, and Jim Haskins discovered his left cheek had been cut by a piece of brick chipped away by one of the bullets. He sank down, breathing heavily, and saw that back at the saloon a few customers had eased outside to see what was going on. But the ambushers were gone, and not sighting Jim Haskins crouched down along the darkness of the brick wall, they went back to the business of drinking.

With the help of his cane, he struggled erect, and managed a wan smile. "Can't prove it wasn't anything more than an attempted holdup. But Elliott'll be one of those in court tomorrow, and he just might be surprised to see me there."

The efforts to get a jury had taken over two weeks, and when court convened the next morning, it was with only eleven people seated in the jury box. During this time over a thousand veniremen had been examined, which meant about every eligible citizen in Cheyenne, to find all but eleven turned down by both the defense and prosecution. This had been explained in an aside to Jim Haskins by another spectator, and then the voice of the Johnson County prosecutor silenced the courtroom:

"Your honor, I move to dismiss the case!"

Immediately the defense in the person of Judge VanDevanter countered with, "I object, your honor, on the grounds that a *nolle prosequi* would leave my clients open to further prosecution."

"Yes, yes," the judge agreed with a reluctant grimace, "as there has been no trial, the constitutional ban against double jeopardy cannot be invoked. What you need, gentlemen, is another juror."

Back in the courtroom on one of the oaken benches, Jim Haskins took in the invaders seated up front. He stared at Joe Elliott and a couple of other stock detectives, with the attention of these men centered on the proceedings before them. And the realization came to Jim Haskins that even if Joe Elliott or the others were behind what had happened last night, the truth of it would never come out. As for this trial, for all intents and purposes it was over. He lingered there until a juror had been picked out of the crowd and sworn in, and then he eased along the bench to find a door and leave the courthouse.

It was an embittered Jim Haskins who caught the afternoon train to Casper, and from there to secure other transportation, a stagecoach. Once he was clear of Casper and on the northward road, he knew that before the day was over, there'd be a long-awaited glimpse of the Big Horns.

"Somehow they've always made me think of Corrie. Just hope she'll welcome me back."

Where Cheyenne, the capital city of Wyoming, had grown, the cow town of Buffalo seemed a lesser place to Jim Haskins. Some of the business places had closed down, he couldn't help noticing as the stagecoach came clattering down onto Main Street, bounced across the bridge passing over Clear Creek, and halted along the wide facade of the Occidental Hotel.

It was at the Occidental Hotel that he secured lodging. And after getting rid of a lot of trail dust and after a change of clothing, he set out in his hobbling walk through the lesser streets of the town. Finally he cleared a large oak tree and came upon the Middletons' two-storied gabled house with the shed and carriage house out back. With eager expectancy he brought a hand rapping against the front door as with the other he removed his hat.

"Yes?" came an inquisitive response from a woman he'd never seen before.

"I'm here to see Corrie."

"No Corrie living here. Oh, you must be looking for the Middletons' daughter. Sorry, mister, but they moved away."

"Away?" His face registering his disappointment, he asked where they had moved, and was told that the Middletons were now residing in San Francisco.

The next few days proved to be difficult ones for Jim Haskins. He looked up people that had befriended him before, and was told more of what had happened in Johnson County. Sometimes on his walks there arose in him the expectancy of seeing Corrie come around some corner. It was here in Buffalo that he knew for certain there could never be another woman for him. So his immediate response was to fire off a telegram to San Francisco:

This time his wire got through as days later Jim

Haskins received one in return, which contained only two words above her name.

"Please Come."

A few months later they were married, and they never did return to Buffalo. Though oftentimes there were bittersweet remembrances of how it had been in Johnson County.